I0742999

Shape Shifting 201
The Hellkitten Chronicles
Book Two

By

Viola Grace

Imara made it through her first term without too many issues, but now that she is in the second term, a magic-draining fiend is stalking the students, and her familiar is bored with guiding her through the early stages of magic. He has taken to giving her misinformation to see if she can use her own judgments. It is a challenge she doesn't really need.

XIA agents are taking courses at the college, and one of them ends up next to Imara during her ethics course. A few conversations lead to a lunch date, and now, she must determine if a social life is worth more than her scholastic one.

Mr. E just likes going on lunch dates. The servers swoon over his cute fuzziness. He is no help at all.

Chapter One

The persistent tapping on her nose and lips brought Imara out of a sound sleep. She spluttered. "What?"

You are going to be late for your first day of winter term. You have forty-five minutes to shower, get dressed, eat, and get across the campus. The close-range kitten face was cross-eyed as he smacked her face with his tiny paw again.

Damnit.

Exactly. Forty-four. The clock is ticking, and you don't know time magic yet. Get rolling.

Imara got up and dumped Mr. E to the floor, stumbling past him to her bathroom. He might be six inches tall, but he was right. She needed to get moving.

Brushing her teeth in the shower caused a soap and toothpaste confusion. It was enough of an issue to wake her up completely, and she left her room with a wet head and a disgruntled kitten five minutes later. He was not a fan of her lack of enthusiasm for a hairdryer.

Reegar had a travel mug of coffee waiting for her. He handed it to her with a jaunty bow. "Your pastry is in the box on the counter."

"Thanks. Immit Hall would have to be on the other end of the freaking campus."

"You will make it. I have seen you run to beat Bara to the remote control. She made your coffee."

Imara wanted to snark at him, but the blueberry pastry was taking up her mouth. She grabbed a second, checked her bag and that she was wearing shoes, and had actually gotten dressed. Some nightmares didn't need to be dragged into reality.

She jammed the second pastry between her jaws, checked for Mr. E, and charged out the door with her coffee cup in her hand.

The first course of the winter term was Shape Shifting 201. It was just the thing to bring misery to a Monday morning.

She jogged and chewed her way through the campus, the mild weather was the gift of the weather mages. It was always temperate if on the cool side.

The coffee was screamingly hot, and the sudden pulse in her lips confirmed that pain was as good as caffeine to wake her up.

Imara finally made it to Immit Hall with three minutes to spare. She found the lecture hall and sat at one of the four available tables. She smiled and nodded as Mesook Mnara waved at her. They had shared the financial-planning class last term, and Mesook had mentioned her desire to take this course.

Imara pulled out her notebook and pencil. She surmised that Mesook had made it off the waiting list.

She took a final slurp from her thermal mug, sealed it, and tucked it into a side pocket of her bag. When she straightened, the instructor wandered in.

Mr. E whispered in her mind. *Well spotted. That isn't a normal lynx.*

The cat paced back and forth, getting closer to the tables and the very still students.

The mage snarled and swiped at the students, one by one. Imara looked at the incoming paw and extended her own hand to meet it.

At the moment of impact, the lynx

changed into a man wearing loose, dark, cotton clothing and a smile. "Well done, Ms. Mirrin. I was told to watch out for you."

"By whom?"

The instructor chuckled. "I will leave you guessing on that matter."

He turned and walked in front of the class of seven. "Hello, I am Magus Korian Yassur. You may call me Instructor Korian."

He faced them and nodded to Imara. "So, what did you see that they didn't?"

"Your form was too large, you made eye contact with more than one of us, there were no postures or behaviours visible that would have indicated you were threatened or hunting. Simply put, you were not acting like a cat."

With every phrase, his eyebrows raised a little higher. "Well, that is encouraging. Are the rest of you aware of what she just pointed out?"

Mesook raised her hand.

"Yes?"

"She pointed out that the shape isn't enough. If you want to be convincing, you have to know the animal you want to become."

Korian nodded. "Correct. This course is partially about the magic you will need to know but mostly about how to research what you need to be convincing."

He gestured, and the lights dimmed. "Let's see what happens when folks get it wrong. If you cannot stand thinking about the errors, this course may not be for you."

Imara watched as an image was projected on the walls behind the instructor.

The picture of the twisted creature lying on the ground was difficult to make out until she located the fingers and worked her way back to the arms. It was a combination of dog, cat and a bit of fish, overlaid on a human structure.

"This was a student two years ago, who had not decided on the beast she wanted to change into. In this very building, she twisted into this and passed away. Her lack of clarity cost her her life."

The light flared, and another image was displayed. A bureau was sitting quietly against the wall. Imara stared, and slowly, a wave of horror overtook her. The pattern in the wood was that of a face, screaming in agony.

"This student chose this form as a joke, but as it was inert, he was found ten days after his transformation. He was in the main hall of his dorm, and no one noticed him."

Imara winced.

"Here is a student who wanted to play with size. He was eaten by his roommate's familiar."

A dead rat was on the floor with blood smears around it.

"Another who wanted to take the form of a large animal but chose the wrong location for transformation."

An elephant trunk flopped out of what seemed to be a broom closet.

Two students got up and left the class.

"Good. That narrows the field. Now, the form you need to build toward should be comfortable, sensible, and of a reasonable size."

Korian walked around the room as the lights came up. "Now, we are going to discuss the anatomy of a shape shift. Many folks think that it is a painless process, but you are reshaping skin, muscle, ligaments, and bone, not to mention the burning itch of growing fur."

He paced around, lithe and restless. "To shift your shape, you need to know how long the claws must be, how many feathers and in what configuration. Instinct will not guide you here. You are designed to be human."

He took a deep breath and centred himself, facing them. "The first things we will learn are simple shifts. They are easily confused with glamour, but we are physically changing the hair, skin, and eye colour. Until you shift back, you will look like someone else."

Korian's smile was full of anticipation. "Now, let's learn about what makes the pigment in your hair."

Imara felt Mr. E settle on her feet, and there was quite a bit of snuffling and snoring as she listened to the instructor for hours.

She took copious notes and asked questions along with the other students. When the class was over, her mind was groaning and she wanted to get started on a few small attempts at magic under her belt. After the last few weeks between semesters, she was more than eager to start again.

When she got ready to stand, Mr. E clawed his way up her body and sat proudly on her shoulder. *You seemed to enjoy the class.*

The instructor was watching as she stood, and there was something in his gaze that indicated he wanted to speak to her.

She walked up to him with her familiar digging into one shoulder and her bag pulling on the other. "Instructor Korian, thank you for the class. I am eager to get started."

He smiled. "Ms. Mirrin, I have been briefed on your situation. I must say, that given your family history, I was surprised to see you in my course."

"Why is that?"

"It is not the sort of thing that your brothers have shown an interest in. I went to school with your eldest brother."

His expression made more sense to her now.

"Ah, I don't have anything in common with my siblings. I have only met one of them that I am aware of."

"I thought you had... I mean the family appears very aware of you."

Imara smiled. "They may be, but I am not aware of them. So, I am looking forward to the next class. You are an engaging instructor."

Korian's dark cheeks flushed. "Thank you. You have an aura of power that makes it hard to concentrate on my words."

Imara blinked rapidly. "Um..."

"And there I go again." He smiled slightly. "I will see you next week."

"Right. Thanks again for the lecture. It left me with definite food for thought." She nodded and left the lecture hall.

He is attracted to you.

She snorted. "Yeah. I got that much. I

am guessing it has more to do with my father's family than with me personally."

The long hike across the quad was just what she needed to clear her mind. Knowing that there was food waiting in the fridge to make a sandwich put a spring in her step.

You mustn't sell yourself short. You are an attractive woman, and if I were a thousand years younger and in a human form again, I would have seduced you already.

"Like hell. I have a plan, and you and other guys don't fit into it. There is time enough for that sort of thing when I finish school and have my own shop."

You really do have a focus, don't you?

"I have worked on it for over a decade. This is my path, and I am going to walk it. Stupidity with men can come later."

She heard him chuckle in her mind.

She kept her echo from him. She wasn't in the habit of dating mass murderers, so he would have been off her list regardless of his own inclinations. Her dear little familiar just wasn't her type.

Chapter Two

With a sandwich and coffee at her side, she hit the library with a vengeance. Reegar was helpful in finding the books that were on her syllabus, but she still needed some basic anatomy information, and for that, she had to decide what she wanted to become.

She sat back and exhaled, looking at Mr. E, asleep on the *Tome of Transformation*. "So, should I be a cat? Dog? Land squid?"

He opened one eye. *You need to pick something you have always wanted to be.*

"I just wanted to be a proper mage."

Go to the roof, listen to the wind, and

close your eyes. Think of the impulse you want to have, and that is your shape. Got it?

"You are exceptionally smug for someone who licks their own backside." Imara got to her feet and, nevertheless, did as he said.

She passed Reegar and headed for the stairs that would take her to the roof.

"Did Bara speak to you?"

Imara paused. "No."

"There is a term mixer that she wanted to drag you to. She mentioned that you should eat, as drinking might be involved."

"Oh. Right. I had a sandwich."

He smiled. "Good."

She nodded and watched the spectre walk into the library to enjoy touching the books again. It was one of the perks that the dead felt being near her. She made them nearly human again.

Imara smirked as she walked up the

stairs. She leaked magical energy and no one complained. It was a nice side effect of being the seventh child of a seventh child from a family who had a lot of necromancers in it. Power across the planes of existence seemed to be a river that had found an estuary in her.

By the time she made it onto the roof, she had her mind back on the task at hand. She wanted to concentrate and let the world around her speak, but all she could hear were the chattering of students on the ground.

She walked to the rail and looked down, focusing on the feel of the wind and the scent of the air. Lifting her head, she looked at the treetops, and a slow smile crossed her lips.

She relaxed and let her senses guide her. She turned her head when she heard noises and noted the pattern that her motions were taking on. The more relaxed she was, the more birdlike she became.

With a deep sigh, she made up her mind. If it had to be a raptor, it had to be a raptor. She just needed to figure out which one.

She skipped back into the library, picked out a book on bird transformations and walked back to the table where Mr. E still had his little black kitten nose covered with his tail. He was a ball of fluff.

She set the book down firmly, and he jumped, hissing and bouncing until he fell off the table.

Her giggles lasted until he climbed her jeans to regain his position on the table.

With a gentle grip, she scooped him up and placed him back in his nap spot. "You could have just asked me to pick you up."

You could have set that book down quietly. So, have you decided?

"I did, but you aren't going to like it." She lifted the book and directed the cover to where he could see it. *Raptors of the Magical World.*

He sighed and cleaned one of his paws. *I thought so. You have a definite predatory air about you.*

"I do not."

He gave her a bland look through his tilted eyes and walked toward the edge of the table.

She snagged him in midair and set him back in his place.

He gave her a smug look. *See?*

"Yes, I see, but I didn't catch you with my feet. That is what I am looking into."

He resumed his bath time while she started flipping through the images of birds and their descriptions of how they had been linked to the magical world.

She didn't know what she was looking for, but she would know it when she found it.

She was nearly to the end of the book when she stopped. "Huh. That is... well... it's definitely a bird."

Mr. E sat up and walked over, peeping over her arm. *Good choice. Strong, powerful, intelligent, and associated with an ancient goddess. Well done, Imara.*

She took in the image of the griffin vulture and sighed. "Right. Time to get going on my anatomy lessons."

Bara's voice sounded behind her. "Oh no. You are coming with me."

Imara turned to look at her. "Did I promise I would go to this?"

"Yes. A week ago. I even got it in writing."

"Damn."

"Indeed. Now, get dressed, or I will use my new makeover spell, and I can't guarantee the results."

That was enough to send Imara scrambling to her room to put on jeans and a dark shirt, brush her hair, and apply a slash of lip gloss.

She returned to the study area a few minutes after she had left it. "Right. Ready."

Bara looked her over and sighed. "Right. Well, you made an effort, so let's go."

Halfway to the door, Imara turned back and called out, "Mr. E, are you coming?"

No, watching young mages get drunk is a memory I will keep in the past. If you need me, call on me.

"Right. Have a nice night and take it easy on the public bathing. The cute gets creepy really fast."

He let out a small coughing noise, and she grinned.

She turned back to Bara. "Come on, let's get this over with."

Bara linked arms with her and hauled her out into the brisk evening air.

They walked for a few minutes when Imara asked Reegar Hall's Resident Advisor, "So, why are we doing this again?"

"Because you need to make connections of the social variety, Imara. Getting your grades isn't enough. When you leave college, you are going to need more than books. You will need folks you can call upon who have different specialities."

"So, this is mercenary?"

"Purely. Fun is incidental. You need to be seen having fun, and it is just that... an appearance of fun. Laugh, dance, enjoy yourself. Even two hours out might have benefits down the road."

"Wow. You are really selling this." Imara smirked. "What is your speciality, by the way?"

"I am still deciding. Reegar isn't in any hurry to turn me out, and I get a discount as long as I am resident there, so I am taking advantage of it."

Imara chuckled. "He likes the company."

"So do I. The last few months have been very alive in the Hall."

"For us you mean? Everybody else around there has punched through the veil a long time ago."

Bara grinned. "For us. The rumour is that Reegar has agreed to take in a few more students, but he is going to be very precise about who he lets in."

"Of course. It is his home, and he is in much better control now than he was last summer."

"That is due to you."

"Well, a side effect of me." She chuckled. "So, where are we going again?"

"To a party at the Echo Hall. There will be food, drink, and party magic. I just hope they don't mix the three."

Imara giggled and kept up with Bara as they made their way across the increasingly congested quad toward a building filled with light and music.

Her mind was filled with the details of what she needed to learn about flying as she met folks, shook some hands, and avoided others.

When she felt she had introduced herself to about sixty percent of the partygoers, she eased away from the crowd and analyzed the party.

Bara was speaking with a group of senior classmates, so Imara was free to scan the room at large. She spotted three people in a matter of seconds she was probably related to on one side of her family or another. Running into cousins and such hadn't really occurred to her. Sure, she knew that at least four of her brothers were still at the college, but the more distant relatives hadn't entered her consciousness.

The tingle of magic got her attention, and she turned to the doors that led to a wide patio. Not one to ignore a display of enchantment, she wandered outside and obtained a soda from a young woman sitting behind a makeshift bar.

"Are you a second-year?"

Imara blinked at the sudden question from behind her. She turned toward the man who asked it and shook her head. "No. I am not."

He grinned. "Excellent. Come with me. I need an assistant for the demonstration."

"I don't recall volunteering." She sipped at her orange soda.

"Would you please assist me in a demonstration of physical magic?"

"Who are you?"

The woman at the bar leaned forward, her blond braids with their bright ties swinging as she moved. "He is the light enchantments professor. Professor Breedwell."

Imara looked at his dark features and the amused sparkle in his brown eyes.

"Sure."

He didn't press his luck. He took her hand and led her to an open tent where folks were lounging and engaged in casual magic. It was a bit beyond bending spoons, but they had to get up and get their own beverages, so the magic was for entertainment only.

"We have a volunteer!"

The crowd cheered. Imara pasted a nervous grin on her features and approached the makeshift stage.

The chair was ready for her, and a cursory check with a diagnostic spell told Imara that there was nothing magical about the carved wood.

"Please, miss, have a seat."

Imara took her seat and settled in.

"Now, miss, we just met out near the bar."

"Correct."

"Your name is..."

"Imara Mirrin."

"Well, I am Professor Breedwell, and tonight, we are going to learn about the details possible in physical magic."

The group clapped politely, but there was an air of anticipation to it.

The professor cast a warding spell, and that gave Imara the first inkling that the group didn't want to be disturbed.

"Now, we are going to see what use can be made of household objects."

Imara quirked her lips. "Should I be nervous?"

He smirked. "Yes."

Extension cords whipped around her wrists and held her tight. She took a deep breath and looked around the room for anyone who would keep this from getting out of hand. All the living faces were eager and nearly trembling with anticipation.

The faces of the spectres in the room were more concerned, and as her tension rose, so did her power output. They went from barely visible to solid, smiling at her as they slowly approached.

Words weren't necessary. If they ever wanted to see her back at Echo Hall, they needed to intervene.

"Professor Breedwell, these restraints are highly inappropriate."

He chuckled. "Don't worry. I do this every term. You won't remember a thing."

"We will." Five spectres stepped toward him and smiled.

"How did you get past the wards?" The professor looked irritated and nervous.

"We were already inside. This is a really bad idea, Poul." A woman in a delicate lacey gown with her hair twisted up and held by a series of carved fans smiled brightly.

"Do I know you?"

"Your grandfather did. Very well in fact. Did he ever get that mole on his lower back taken care of?"

The professor looked ill. "You are a ghost."

"Spectre. There is a difference."

A man in the audience called out. "What is the difference?"

Imara felt the tug on her senses as one of the spectres reached out and elevated him above the audience with the flick of his fingers. The man smiled and murmured. "Magic."

The room rioted with students trying to get away from the spectres who were giving a very detailed example of physical magic. Clothing flew, students flew, and the professor was hung by his ankles from the ceiling.

Imara was still tied to the chair as she watched it all.

The professor finally realized that she had to be related to the events. "Stop it."

"Great. Untie me."

The cords released, and she rubbed

her wrists as she stood up. "They will gradually lose power, but if you want this to cease completely, drop the wards. I need another soda."

She felt the wards come down, and the crowd scattered. It seemed that this private party was over.

She gave the female spectre a small nod. "Thank you."

"Our pleasure, mistress. I hope this experience does not stop you from visiting again."

"Oh, no. This has been very entertaining. I believe you can put the professor down now."

The woman smiled slowly. "May I play with him a little?"

The professor's flushed face drained of colour.

"I think you can save that for another day. If he returns here, send word to me at Reegar Hall, and I can come and add some life to the events."

The spectres in the chamber grinned.

"Thank you, again. Please enjoy the party."

With that little pleasantry done with, Imara headed out to get another soda.

This party isn't so bad after all. She was grinning the entire way back to Bara's side.

Chapter Three

"You were right. I am having fun." Imara grinned at Bara.

The waves of shock and scandal were making their way through the crowd.

Bara glanced at her, saw the grin, and excused herself from her conversational group. "What happened?"

"A professor asked me to volunteer, but the situation turned unwholesome, so I asked him to stop, and when he wouldn't, I sought alternative assistance."

One of the spectres walked into the room and bowed elegantly to the ladies before striding to his portrait and examining the plaque below.

Bara sighed, "You released some ghosts."

"No, I let some spectres enjoy the party. There is a difference." Imara chortled.

"You could have casted for help."

"Nope. There was a heavy ward around the area. I am fairly sure this wasn't the first time, but the audience was putting out some severely pervy vibes. I decided that I didn't want to play anymore."

"Do you want to stay?"

"Sure. The spectres are out and enjoying themselves, the display was broken up, and the professor had to beg for freedom. It is quite the party."

Bara sighed. "I am glad you got loose, but try and keep out of trouble."

"I try, but trouble finds me."

"Stop wearing a neon sign."

"Imara! I am so happy to see you." Mesook rushed up to her and linked arms. "You wouldn't believe what just happened."

Imara nodded to Bara and let her classmate drag her away. "What?"

"Well, there are ghosts at the party. Real thinking and speaking ghosts."

Imara twisted her lips. "When they are mages and attached to a structure, they are spectres."

"Right. Well, a necromancer set them to attack one of our professors."

Imara blinked. "*Our* professor?"

"Yes. He is teaching the ethics class."

"Oh, good grief, he said he was light enchantments. That man has no business teaching ethics." Imara snorted.

"You know him?"

She chuckled. "We have met."

Mesook led her out to the rear gardens where music was playing, and light streamed from dozens of enchanted illuminated globes that bobbed and levitated over the partygoers.

"So, Imara..."

Imara felt her eyebrows lift. "Yes?"

"Have you chosen your beast yet?"

She blinked in surprise. "What?"

"Your beast, your shape-shifting animal. You are going to be a cat, aren't you? I mean you have one, so it is an easy transition."

"Uh, I don't think it will be a cat. Why do you ask?"

Mesook's expression was bashful. "I didn't want to pick the same creature and have you outdo me. I am going to try a family icon."

"Well, I am pretty sure you are safe. I don't have a family icon to change into."

Mesook smiled, and she sighed. "Right. So, Asian dragon for me then."

Imara was startled. "Are you sure?"

"Are you afraid I will get better marks than you?"

"No, I am afraid you will lose control and get stuck. That is a lot of square footage. They are huge. The instructor recommended changing into a creature nearly your own size."

"I think you are nervous about my choosing a more impressive beast than yours. You keep your own council."

Imara nodded. "Fine. I will. I wish you luck with your creature. Remember, if you do want to practice, do it in a large area."

Mesook snorted and walked away, her shining black curtain of hair swinging against her lower back. The competitive side of her was a bit of a surprise. She had seemed perfectly fine in the herbology class.

She honestly hoped that they only had the two classes together.

Shrugging, Imara headed inside, passing a group of young women gathered around what looked to be a second-year student who was sobbing. Imara passed them and avoided staring. She found Bara, inclined her head, and mentioned that she was leaving.

"So soon?"

"I have had enough fun for one evening." She grimaced. "I want to leave before someone gets the plague or something."

"Ouch. Do you mind if I stay here?"

"Nope. Go ahead. I have some more zoological studying to do, and I am not sure what Mr. E is getting up to in my absence. He was a little too happy to be rid of me for the night."

Bara chuckled. "Thanks for coming out. See you at the hall."

Imara nodded and headed off, walking upstream through the crowd still entering the party. The night air had cooled considerably, and she shivered in the shock from the warm building to the cold quad.

She smiled slightly as she passed a few spectres near buildings in her path.

They nodded in greeting and didn't ask her to speak to them. It was a politeness that she appreciated, as talking to spectres when the living were around was frowned on.

Approaching Reegar Hall, she could feel the magic pulsing inside the walls. Entering, she clapped a hand over her mouth as bubbles filled the air and appeared to be coming from the study area.

Magus Reegar was waving his hands with precise motions, and Mr. E was leaping around catching the magical bubbles that were floating out of a small portal.

Imara kept her hand over her mouth as her little familiar pounced from bubble to bubble, blinking as they exploded before he sat on his hind legs with his front paws stroking the air to catch the next bubble.

She must have made a sound because

Reegar paused before resuming with a smile.

"He is giving the kitten in him a night to itself. If you are home, you will be pressed into tummy scratching detail after this."

Imara grinned. "Right. I will be on it. First, I am doing some research on my shape shifting. He can jump on my lap when he wants my attention."

"Excellent. I think he has taken in enough power from the bubbles. He will probably want a nap and then a cuddle."

She chuckled and went through the sparkling bubbles, taking up her position at the desk and getting back to her studies. Choosing a vulture as her beast was going to be difficult socially, but it felt right. She just had to find the details that would confirm her gut feeling. Time to study.

An hour later, with a purring kitten in

her lap, she stared at her free hand and tried to compare the visible structure to that of a bird. It wasn't that different, but there would have to be the hollow nature taken into account during the shift. Unless she were a vulture nine feet tall, she would need to work on mass dispersal and return. It was more complicated than she wanted to go in her first form, but things were what they were. She would have to find a way to become her beast.

A sleepy voice whispered in her mind. *Why is it so important that you get it right the first time?*

"Because, Mr. E, I am making a form that flies. If I screw this up, I am going to be pavement pizza."

Keep rubbing my tummy.

She chuckled and pushed aside her diagrams and sketches. Her watch pinged, and it was time for bed.

"Well, I guess that I have to head for

bed. There is an ethics course in the morning, and I want to be bright eyed and ... well, that's it. No tail required."

She scooped the sleepy kitten up and put him on the table. "Did you want to stay out here tonight?"

He purred in response.

"Fine, you know how to get in when you need to."

He purred again, his tail covering his nose.

She snickered and headed for bed. If he wanted to curl up with her, he could open the door. Nothing could stop a familiar from getting to his charge.

Gathering herself, she stepped into the ethics class and took her seat, not looking at Professor Breedwell. Mr. E sat upright on her shoulder, and he kept quiet.

She glanced at the other students and was a little surprised at the fullness of the course as well as the variety of ages represented. It seemed that everybody needed an ethics course now and then. Her familiar got a few stares, and several cooing sounds. He was remarkably cute.

Five more students arrived after she did, and when they were seated, the professor straightened. "Ladies and gentlemen, I welcome you to your first Magical Ethics class. We will learn all of the legal and moral ramifications of using and abusing your enchantments, as well as how to minimize the trouble with law enforcement."

Several of the older students chuckled. It was suddenly clear what they were doing there.

Imara smiled. She was in a class taught by a pervert, and she was surrounded by law enforcement. Well, that was certainly a stroke of luck. She took out her book and pen, settling in for the lecture. It was *definitely* a pretty good day.

Mr. E kept his own council during the lecture aside from the occasional snort when the professor said that the vulnerability of those you were with always needed to be considered.

Imara raised her brows at the professor, and he blushed. It appeared he didn't practice what he preached.

What did I miss?

She bit her lip and tried to focus. *Nothing. I handled it.*

Then there should not have been anything to handle. I will check your memories.

Before she could do more than shift in her seat, he had found the details of the party, and his fur fluffed up. *That kind of charm was slimy when I was a mage. Now, his work is just tacky.*

Don't do anything.

What can I do? I am just a kitten.

There was a dark intent beneath

those innocent words, and Imara frowned until he calmed down and his fur resumed its normal level of fluff.

By the time the lecture concluded, she had ten pages of notes regarding historical events which pointed to skewed ethics, as well as her assignment for the following week.

She scooped her work into a pile when the class was over and headed for the door. The man who had been sitting next to her paused and smiled. "Hi."

She looked at the man whose bearing screamed law enforcement, and she nodded. "Hello."

"Since we will be sitting next to each other, I thought I would introduce myself. I am Argus Dencroft."

She juggled her work and extended her hand. "Imara Mirrin."

He grinned and shook her hand. Mr. E growled softly.

"Is he your familiar?"

"Yeah."

"I have never seen a bound familiar before. Is he inherited?"

She blinked. The class was emptying around them. "Uh, yeah. He is. Mr. E, this is Argus. Argus, this is Mr. E."

She shifted her grip on her papers and books. "I haven't met a griffon before."

He stared at her, his dark gold eyes wide in his tanned face. He was gold and white from head to toe. His soul screamed that he was a griffon, and she was very attentive to souls.

"You... how do you know that?"

She smiled. "It is a conversation for another time. Right now, I need to put this paperwork down before I drop it. I am feeling a tectonic shift will occur at any moment."

He paused and then took her books. "Would you care for coffee?"

She blinked. "Um, sure. There is a

nice café about a block away if you don't mind the walk."

He grinned. "I think that meeting you is something I should make time for."

The air went out of her lungs as his features went from interesting to devastatingly handsome. She blinked, blushed, and led the way to the café. Keeping ahead of him was her only way to maintain dignity. Mr. E laughing uproariously in her mind didn't help.

Chapter Four

Imara ordered for them both and waited for the coffee at the end of the counter. When she had their order, she paused a second before a patron shoved their chair back, windmilling their arms as they lost their balance. Imara went around the fall and made it to the table where Argus waited. Mr. E balanced carefully and chuckled when another patron wasn't as graceful.

"That was lucky."

She smiled. "You don't say."

"Yeah, if that had been me, I would be wearing the coffee." He sipped and smiled. "Perfect. How did you guess?"

"You looked like a *one and one* kind

of guy to me."

He chuckled. "Funny."

"I know. So, why are members of the XIA here and taking courses?"

"We need to keep up our education if we want to be promoted. Ethics is a fairly easy course for us as we already have the training." He nodded to her paperwork. "You take thorough notes."

"Oh. Thanks. I would rather take down too much than not enough." She sipped at her ridiculously complicated latte.

"How did you know about my form?"

She blinked. "Ah, that. Right. Well, I have a primary focus that lets me see what is behind the physical."

He frowned. "I don't understand."

"I was a death keeper."

He still looked at her blankly.

"I see souls."

"Ghosts?"

She chuckled. "Not unless you are already dead. No. I see the motivating intelligence and energy that a living being possesses."

"Oh, so you can see through glamours?"

"Yup. That too." She gave him a small smile. "Isn't it weird for so many XIA agents to be in one class at the same time?"

He sipped at his cup. "Yes, this is very good coffee."

She nodded. "Right. So, how are you enjoying the college?"

Argus smiled. "Today has been a great day. It beats going to work."

"Where do you work?"

"Redbird City."

She set her cup down. "No way."

"Have you been there?"

She shook her head, "No, but it is in my business plan."

"You have a business plan?" He settled back in his chair and smiled.

"Of course. Why would I go to school if I didn't know what I would do afterward? I have done marketing studies, completed a business class, and am getting the certifications that I need to get my license for public magic." She ticked them off on her fingers.

He stared at her in surprise. "How old are you?"

"Nineteen. Well, I will be nineteen in a month."

His shock was evident.

She smirked. "You thought I was older."

"Yes. Yes, I did." He ran a hand through his hair. He sat straight again and seemed to reboot his brain. "What does a death keeper do?"

She smiled and explained how the people of Sakenta City dealt with their mages after physical life had fled. He asked question after question, and she answered them all. It was nice to have someone showing an interest in her talent.

They talked about the way Sakenta used the spectres as a resource for their families, and why it was a waste to ignore that much conscious power floating around. Argus was particularly interested in the fact that the spectres were aware of time passing around them.

Mr. E was sitting on the table, playing with a straw, when he suddenly sat up and yowled.

"Mr. E. What the hell?" She looked at him, and he gave her an unblinking stare with no commentary. Past the cute little ball of black fur, the daylight was turning orange. The afternoon was gone.

"Oh, damn. I am sorry, Argus, but I have to get going." She gathered her books and got to her feet.

"Imara, at least let me walk you home for all of the information you have given me."

Mr. E let out another ear-splitting yowl.

"I don't think that would be a good idea. See you next week in class, Argus. It was great talking with you."

Before he could answer, she bobbed a bow and left the café, Mr. E crawling up her arm as she walked.

Are you going to tell me why I did that?

Don't trust griffins. They have two natures and seldom direct both in the same area.

You are jealous.

He is too old for you.

She laughed the entire way back to Reegar Hall.

Using his calculations, everyone on campus was too old for her. Most weren't accepted until their twenty-first year. She and her twin were exceptions. They may have been separated at birth, but Luken shared her skills with books.

He enjoyed studying as much as he enjoyed spending time with Bara over the holidays.

Having her twin dating a woman three years older wasn't a bad thing, but Bara seemed to have more than Luken Demiel on her mind. If there was a woman with less interest in finishing her scholastic career, Imara hadn't met her. Bara seemed to consider being a permanent student as an occupation. If she could afford it, Imara was cheering her on.

Back home, she checked her schedule for the next few days. She would be busy, but with the intensive classes at one subject per day, she had the next eleven weeks planned out. Classes in the mornings or afternoons, labs and homework in the evenings. It was the same schedule that she had engaged in during the first term, but the compressed classes were going to get exponentially harder.

She went to work on her ethics homework with a bright grin. Next week, she would get to see Argus again.

Her herbology course for second level was a mix of ages. The only folks in first year who qualified for the second course were herself and anyone who passed the exam. As far as she knew, that meant she was the only freshman student in the class. Everyone around her had their eyes on graduating.

Master Limokken was the instructor, and he looked them over before he pronounced, "This course is going to be graded on personal development with the final exam being eighty percent of the marks."

She tensed and listened carefully. Usually, she could get by by doing the homework in advance, but this wasn't going to be the case.

"Weekly, we will delve into different potions and poultices made from herbs. For the exam, you are going to grow your own plants with an eye toward forwarding their magic content. You are going to decide what you want your potion to do, and then, you will find the patch of soil on the campus that has the best magic content and, from there, grow your plants. If you don't start your plants in the next fourteen days, you won't have a sample before the exam. The details are in your course outline, so get to work and call me when you have something you want me to grade you on."

Imara looked around at the shocked faces of her classmates and headed to her workstation, her notebook in hand. She wanted to create a caffeine substitution for mornings, and this was as good a time as any.

With most of the other students still

figuring out what they wanted to do, Imara and a couple of others got to work.

Mr. E supervised and watched her work from his perch on her shoulder. *You have come a very long way in a very short time.*

That is what I intended to do.

I know where the soil is. There was a smug tone to his voice.

She smiled slightly and sniffed at some lemon zest. *I believe I do as well.*

Where do you think it is?

Under the rim of the edge of the wave site. Since the campus is built on the site of an invading wave of magic, it makes sense that there would be some stored under the edge.

Sensible, but a little too literal.

What?

Where do you think magic is spilled over and over without dispersing?

The duelling ground?

See? You figured it out.

I don't know that the quality of magic spilled would be useful. I need magic that hasn't taken a shape yet.

Mr. E's rich tone was amused, *Are you sure I can't misdirect you?*

Pretty sure. I am going to find the site of the wave and get the soil there.

Good.

I thought you weren't supposed to misdirect me.

I would have stopped you before you followed my guidance. If I don't push you now and then, you will become dependent on me.

It was sound thinking. If they were ever separated and she needed to defend herself, waiting for him to tell her what to do might cost her life. Thinking for herself was a good habit to keep.

After two hours, the instructor made his rounds, and he checked on the potions. He looked over her notes and the progress she was making with the mortar and pestle and nodded. "Trouble waking up?"

"Something like that."

"Watch your ratios. You don't want to have undirected stimulation."

She looked over her notes and added a decimal place to the flower petals. She didn't need a potion that lasted as long as the flowers bloomed; she needed it for a day. With careful deliberation, she added sunflowers to the recipe. She would pass out the moment that the sun went down, but she would be bright and able while it was shining.

Imara worked until nearly the end of the class. With a look at the paste in her mortar, she realized what she wanted to do with it. She made a note in her book and made eye contact with the instructor.

He sauntered over and looked at the mash she was scraping into a jar. "I thought you were aiming for a potion."

"This will have more of a general waking rather than waking my digestive tract. The preparation will be applied to my temples, and that will spread the effect through my brain, or at least, that is the theory."

He nodded. With a flourish, he pulled out a sampling kit. He put a miniscule sample into a tiny flask and added a drop of diagnostic liquid.

"Well, you have magic, you have energy, and you have alertness. I give you a ninety percent for this first assignment."

She nodded and exhaled. "Ten percent because I didn't know what form it would take, right?"

Master Limokken nodded. "Correct. If I didn't know what you were aiming for, it would have been a hundred percent, but you had the word potion at the top of your page."

She blinked. "Right. Thank you, Master Limokken."

"Oh, and your familiar is welcome to help you find the soil. The years have shown that they don't do better than anyone else." He chuckled and left her workstation.

She sighed and set the jar down while she took her equipment to the sink. Mr. E was napping on her notebook, and she finished washing up, bringing everything back to her station and putting it away for the other students who took classes in the lab.

Mr. E was cleaning his paw when she finished, and she gave him a long look. *What is that about?*

One of the others got curious, so I defended your creation. I will accept a can of sardines in gracious tribute.

She stowed the container in her bag, and Mr. E hopped up onto her shoulder. With her station clear, she left the lab and went in search of the source of magic within the college.

Chapter Five

Wild magic usually left a distinct marker on the landscape, but the college didn't have any obvious signs of the wave coming through.

She was looking for the remains of a volcano in what amounted to a mountain range. Imara tried to look casual as she crossed the campus, her senses wide open and looking for a specific trace of something that shouldn't be there. When she only got touches from the population of the college, she pulled her senses back in. She was going to have to do some research, and the best books were home at Reegar Hall. She was lucky that Reegar just happened to have collected everything she needed.

Smirking to herself, she turned in place and started to walk back the way she had come. The collision with the man immediately behind her knocked her back and made Mr. E hiss.

She blinked rapidly. "I am so sorry. I changed my mind about my destination."

The man brushed at his clothing, and he nodded. "No harm done."

She paused and stared at another of her brothers. "Right. Well, excuse me."

She stepped around him and his friends, heading back toward home without looking back. She knew what she would see. His eyes were the same shade as hers, his hair was a touch darker, and his jaw was stronger, but he was definitely one of her siblings. She didn't know which one he was, so she kept going until she was in the hall with the door closed behind her.

I thought you liked Luken.

I do, I just don't know how the others feel about me. Luken is the seventh son of the seventh son; he has the power he needs. The others might not be so charitable.

Right. Good plan. Your mother's family eventually became more interested in learning than destruction, but the Demiels have always been on the violent side.

She headed for the kitchen. *Were they on your list, too?*

I was getting there. The original Deepfords were a definite bunch of black souls, using demonic energies to gain power, land, and dominion over other mages.

Right. Anyway, I need to study to find the oldest structures on the campus. Any idea where I should start?

Start with the college memorial edition. It should have the list of oldest books.

She smiled and spoke out loud. "Excellent. I will start there."

He nuzzled her neck as she dropped her bag on the study table and helped her make a few choices from the library.

"What are you looking for, Imara?" Reegar walked in and watched her molest his collection.

"I am looking for a record of the oldest building at the college."

"Why?"

"I need to find the most magical soil on the property and use it for herbology. I don't want to use the mage's battlegrounds because there is focus and intent in that magic. I need wild magic. I want to find the source of the wave that sprouted at the school."

Reegar cocked his head. "There have been hundreds of attempts to find the source. It always evades those seeking it."

"Maybe they just haven't asked nicely."

He chuckled. "Perhaps that is it. I have a few books on the search."

"Look them up, please. I will need to start at the beginning if I am going to find the soil I am looking for."

Magus Reegar, spectre for decades and master of the house, headed off to find her the books.

While she waited, she got Mr. E his sardine and got herself some crackers and cheese. His mind broadcasted happiness that only occurred when the kitten in him had full control.

She set out her notebooks and took out the alertness poultice. She sniffed it a few times and enjoyed the sensation of a waking mind.

Reegar came in with armloads of books trailing behind him, riding on a cushion of magic. Some of them looked older than the building she was in.

She looked at the stack set before her, and she took a deep breath, running her hands down the spines.

"What are you doing?"

"Trying to see if I get lucky." The faintest tingle ran through her left hand, and she pried the book out of the pile.

Reegar snorted. "That is a fictional account of the college. It was a history created by a previous student."

Imara grinned and settled in her chair. "Those are the best kind of stories. If I can get a clue, it will be worth the read."

He blinked and wandered back to the stacks of the library, phasing through a few of the shelves as he passed.

Mr. E climbed her leg and used her to boost himself onto the table. When he had curled up in a ball, she smirked and started reading.

The book was a novel nearly a hundred years old and written by an L.

Ganger. *Hunted Moonlight* was the tale of a woman with blended bloodlines who was being pursued by a man with demon blood. They were both at the school, one as a student and one as an instructor. It was an amazing read.

She sniffled and sobbed during the book, finally getting to the ending where the couple forced their families' agreement by consummating their love in tasteful and obscure terms in the chancellor's garden, under a pear tree.

When she read the reference to the garden, she felt the tingle on her skin again. Right, well, that made sense and was a good place to start.

She set the book back in the pile and went looking for a spell book on diagnostics. If she was looking for the source of magic on the campus, she was going to need a way to prove she had found it.

Bara came home with her arms loaded with supplies. "What are you up to?"

"I am just heading to the lab to make up some magic test strips."

"What?"

"Like an acidity test but for magic."

"Cool. Can I help?" Bara shifted her armloads of books and bags.

"I think you have your hands full. What are you taking this term?"

"Weaving. Magus Reegar said I could use the loom in the attic.

"Do I want to know why he has a loom in the attic?"

Bara grinned. "One of the students he scared away left it behind. I had better drop this stuff up there."

"You do that; I will get started." Imara continued her search, flipping through book after book until she found a few spells and potion recipes that would work. The thumping that was coming from the upper floor was enough indication that Bara wasn't going to be coming down anytime soon.

Reegar appeared at her side. "Would you like advice?"

"Sure. Let me just wake Mr. E up. If I let him sleep in the afternoons, he gets all cranky."

"How can you tell?"

She chuckled and passed the table where Mr. E still snoozed. She shifted the books to one arm and tickled him awake. "C'mon. I actually need you as a familiar."

He stretched, arching his small back with his fluff standing out at all angles. Half of his face fur was flattened, and he had a serious case of bedhead. She bit her lower lip and put him on top of the books with some blank sheets of paper before she headed to the lab.

What are you going to make?

Magic detection strips.

So... I can't shred this stuff?

She grinned and said out loud. "Nope, behave."

Setting up in the lab was fun. Mr. E perched on a tall stool, the books were open in front of her, and Reegar was telling her where to find the ingredients.

"I have never seen anyone combine those spells before."

She wrinkled her nose. "They seem right. Each has bits that I need for this to work."

"What if it blows?"

Imara laughed, "That is what Mr. E is for. He can at least repurpose my spectre so that I don't hang around and pester you. Then, he will go on to the next family member in line for him, or he will head to a different family. Either way, I am prepared for anything."

"I have never met anyone before you that had such a detachment for their life."

"I like being alive; I am just accepting that this isn't all there is." She took a deep breath, checked that she had all her supplies and equipment ready, and started to mix and chant with the white paper neatly settled next to the work area.

Hours went by with only gentle direction from Reegar and method critiques from Mr. E.

The light purple liquid was a small result for such a long effort. "Well, here goes."

With gloved hands, she picked up the small basting brush and painted the paper, front and back. The line with tiny clips was ready to hold the bespelled paper as it dried.

The small bowl of liquid covered twelve pages, absorbed quickly, and when it was used up, the light flashed brilliantly when Imara soaked the bowl and brush in the sink.

"Ouch. Okay, so it is water sensitive. Good to know."

Reegar laughed. "I thought it would

be. A few of your ingredients are thirsty."

She snorted. "I know. I didn't think it would be that abrupt when they touched water."

The rest of the dishes were less violent. She was able to clear all the implements and put them on the drying rack without incident.

She checked the papers' progress, but they were still drying. "I am going to have to warn Bara about that."

"She has hung a few experiments out to dry, so I am sure she will be understanding." Reegar looked toward the line but kept his distance.

"I will have to remember to put gloves on before I move them." She muttered it to herself and double-checked her notes before closing her book and the others.

When everything was ready, she removed the gloves and draped them over the edge of the sink. "Okay, I think I am done for the night."

Good. It is past your bedtime.

She checked her watch and cursed. "Dammit. Why didn't anyone tell me?"

Reegar inferred her meaning. "You were engaged in creative spell combinations, I haven't seen that kind of enthusiasm in decades."

She muttered as she left the lab, dropped the books off at the study table and headed to bed. If she were lucky, she would get four hours of sleep.

Mr. E followed her, chortling in her thoughts. As she brushed her teeth, he snickered so she *accidentally* splashed him with water, and he hissed and skittered.

She apologized profusely and towelled him dry. She kept the part of her mind that he had casual access to calm with a hint of sympathy. The rest of her was snickering.

She only had one class left in the

short week, so as long as she could get through the first class in household spell work, she would be fine.

She was snickering at herself as she fell asleep. She was going to get her butt kicked.

Chapter Six

"Domestic spell work doesn't involve any fancy chants or noxious potions. You use your mind, your power, and your control over the elements to keep your environment clean and under your control. In my class, it is easy to see the result of your study and focus. Your assignment is either clean, or it isn't." Magus Beelin paced back and forth in front of the rows of desks.

Imara held in her yawns as the instructor went on about what she expected of the class. She sat blinking in surprise when the class got practical in a rush.

"I want each one of you to come here

and try and move this broom."

The class members got to their feet and shuffled to the area that Magus Beelin was pointing to. "Each of you will have thirty seconds to move the broom. Anyone who can do it is guaranteed a passing grade on the first test."

Imara hung back and tried to think of what she knew about telekinetic spells. There weren't any.

The timer chimed, and the first candidate shuffled forward. The mage strained from his place in line and tried to beckon the broom toward them. Nothing.

The next member of the class tried, and there was no success.

The minutes shot past, and soon, Imara was the only student who hadn't tried. The others were all seated and defeated.

The timer started, and Imara asked, "May I move?"

The magus quirked her lips. "Yes."

Imara walked to the broom and brought it back to the magus. The gasps and cries of the shocked students echoed in her ears.

Magus Beelin smiled, "Why did you walk to it?"

"It would have taken more effort to summon it."

At the nodded dismissal, Imara walked back to her seat, ignoring the glares of her classmates.

"That student has just proven a point you need to remember. The magic involved takes just as much from you as doing it by hand. The speed gained is a trade-off for your personal energy. There is nothing as draining as housework, and that includes those who can use an enchantment as well as those who work with their hands."

She set the broom back in its stand. "There are no spells for sweeping. The amount of control would mean you were stuck staring at the broom the entire time. Get one of those vacuuming robots if that is your only concern. If you want to sweep quickly, run a summoning spell for all dirt in your house and direct it to a bucket. That is not the first spell we will be working on, but it is on the list."

Magus Beelin raised her head. "The first spell work we are going to get into is stain removal. You are going to run into all kinds of substances here, and being able to clean your own clothing is important. From now on, come to this class prepared to get filthy so we can all work from the same baseline."

She waved her hands in the air. "Our classes will let you unclog a toilet, repair shattered glass, and get your room ready for your parents to drop in in under a minute. You will feel the strain, but you won't look like a slob."

The class chuckled and then sat back

as the instruction began.

Hours later, Imara packed up her notebooks, put her pencil away and looked in satisfaction at the spot on her t-shirt that had been stained with oil an hour earlier. Spot removal was definitely something she could manage.

As she left her desk, Mr. E resumed his position on her shoulder. *I never learned to do that kind of thing. I guess it would have been useful.*

Learning how to take care of your own environment is always useful.

"Ms. Mirrin." The magus stopped her from leaving.

"Yes, Magus Beelin?"

"You have one hundred percent for the next test. Use the option wisely and study for the subsequent tests. The exam will be particularly taxing, so build up your stamina."

"Yes, Magus. Thank you."

"Don't thank me; you are the one who

figured out manual labour would do the trick better than untrained magic."

"May I still take the test?" She asked cautiously.

The magus's smile was wide. "Hm, you do appreciate the education you are getting here."

"If I don't take the test, Magus Beelin, how will I know if I am ready for the next one?"

"Of course, you can take the test. I will even let you know how you did, but you will still pass, regardless."

"I would rather earn a passing grade."

The magus patted her on the shoulder. "You already did."

Mr. E purred and rubbed his cheek against Imara's. It was a signal to shut up and move along.

"Thank you, Magus. Have a good day."

"Have a good weekend, Mirrin. You have your work cut out for you."

Imara nodded and left the classroom. Removing the small spot of oil had exhausted her, and now that the weekend was looming, she had a nap planned before she tackled her homework.

The knock on her door was persistent.

"What?" Imara sat up and rubbed her eyes.

"Come on, you are getting off campus, and we are going out to dinner. My treat." Bara's voice was desperate.

Imara checked to make sure she still had her clothing on and opened her door. Bara was standing there, hair frazzled and her fingers wrapped in gauze and tape.

"Weaving kicking your ass?" Imara grabbed her shoes and put them on.

"Yes. I don't know how mages have done it for centuries." She sighed and slumped her shoulders.

Imara snickered as she stood. "They

specialize. You are trying to specialize in everything. It isn't always going to work."

Bara groaned. "I know, but I have to try. It is a compulsion to try and get through all the course offerings, so I know where I want to direct my focus in the future."

"Right. Makes sense even if it is a little hard on you. Can I bring Mr. E?"

"We are going to be eating at a sit-down restaurant, so I would suggest you leave him here unless he can go invisible."

Mr. E was stretching on the pillow where he slept. *I can. The question is do I want to go out with two girls who are going to talk about me being cute and fluffy?*

Imara grinned. "Your choice, Mr. E. I want to grab one of those tester packs before we go, Bara. Nothing like a road test out in the real world."

Imara grabbed her bag and headed out of the dorm area, down the stairs, and down the hall to the lab. The vials of test strips that she had cut before her nap were all lined up with wooden pincers rubber banded to their exteriors. She settled one of the vials on the interior pocket of her bag and grinned at Bara. "So, you said it was your treat?"

"Yeah, can you drive? My hands are a little raw."

"Sure. Let's go."

With no sign of her familiar, Imara headed out with Bara and helped her open the car door. Bara acted as navigator, and they cruised through the gates of the college and into the town, resting in the valley below.

They parked in the lot of an Italian style restaurant, and Bara accepted her help getting out of the car. Her hands were in really rough shape.

"Maybe you should go to a medical

centre.”

“They would have a bit of trouble with my injuries. They are all psychosomatic.” Bara made a face.

“What?”

“My fingers got sensitive, so I wrapped them up. I am not actually that injured beyond a few blisters.”

Imara snickered as they headed for the building. “So, you are trying to dissuade yourself?”

“Yup. I know my triggers.”

They waited and then followed a young woman to a booth.

Imara took her menu and looked it over. She casually mentioned, “You seem to have a good grip on your situation.”

Bara grinned and peeked over her menu. “My entire family is nuts. Arming myself by learning what sets me off, what I need to learn, and how I get around my own neurosis is my permanent occupation.”

“Wow... that is... wow.”

“Yeah, I come from a long line of mad mages.” Bara set her menu down. “What about you?”

“Ah, well, you have met my mom.”

“Yeah, that was a little surprising. Explain to me how that is possible again?”

The server came and took their order. Imara ordered lasagne with a side of garlic toast and a salad, Bara opted for spaghetti with meatballs and the same sides.

Once they were sitting with their iced water and the menus were gone, Imara faced the resident advisor of her hall.

“So, why do you want to know the details?”

“I am really curious as to why you don’t know your own mother. I know you told me, but I didn’t pry. I feel like prying today if you are amenable.”

Imara sat back. "Well, from what my mother told me, and what was in my file, the Deepford-Smythes were broke. Plenty of power but no money. The Demiel family had reached the end of their line for interbreeding, so they wanted a powerful bloodline to mix with theirs. Each family had a seventh child program running for extra power, and in the case of the Deepford-Smythes, they didn't discriminate against the females. They counted them all. The chancellor was the seventh member of her family, and my father was the seventh of his. A contract was signed to produce the desired seventh of seven, and they got married. I think you can guess what happened next."

"She wasn't happy."

"Nope. After each child, she was healed, and the next pregnancy commenced. It was dangerous, and she was treated like a farm animal. She hated it.

When Luken and myself were born, the Demiels wanted me discarded as quickly as possible. As the eighth out of the seventh, I wasn't considered lucky. Luken got that particular designation."

Bara wove her fingers together and rested her chin on them with her elbows on the table. "What happened then?"

"My mother's family made arrangements to place me in Sakenta City. Since my mother was planning to divorce my father the moment that the contract was fulfilled, she had a plan for one of the twins. She was surprised that I was a girl but very happy at the same time. An eighth boy would definitely be unlucky, so I was taken away and put into care."

Their salads arrived, and a few minutes were spent as they munched their way through them.

Bara finally mumbled, "This is better than a soap opera. What happened then?"

"She divorced my father and left her seven sons. She took a teaching position at the college and worked her way up the ladder. She became the chancellor of the college by virtue of her skills, her time at the college, and her family."

"So, you grew up alone?"

"No, I grew up in one of the regulated placement homes in Sakenta. Folks have magic there, but no one uses it."

That was enough to redirect Bara's questions. For the rest of their time in the restaurant, Imara explained how she could grow up as she had without using magic until she was an adult.

"So, how is it you were able to qualify for the college?"

"I didn't say I didn't have magic, I just couldn't do the kind of thing that I am learning now. When I was a teen, I got a job at the Memorial Gardens as an apprentice death keeper. Talking to the dead isn't considered magic in Sakenta.

It is necessary."

"This is amazing. You worked a night shift during school?"

"Yeah, it is a good thing that being a death keeper pays well. I was trying to save enough for college."

Bara grinned, "If you are the chancellor's daughter, you get free tuition."

"Only if I am legally claimed. I am not. She is the chancellor, and I am Imara. That is all we need to be, though one of my clients in the Memorial Gardens did send enough money to the college to cover my tuition until graduation. It is another reason I am in a hurry. I want to get into the job market and start using the one thing that I am really good at."

"What is that?"

"Dealing with spectres." She grinned and waved the last bite of lasagne in the air. "Even the master death keeper said he had never seen anything like my talent."

She ate the last bite and leaned back. "Thank you. That was delightful."

"My pleasure. Thank you for driving. So, have you heard about what is going on at the campus?"

"The women turning up powerless?"

"Yeah, that."

Imara scowled. "I thought that was just a rumour."

"Nope. One of the girls was in my enchanted textile class. She can't do anything. She had to go to the dean's office and have her classes suspended until she can use magic again. The weird thing is she doesn't know how it happened. She was at a party, blacked out, and woke up without the slightest drop of magic."

Imara shivered. "That is creepy. Didn't anyone see anything?"

"No one has reported anything. For now, they are treating it like a frat prank, but I am going to keep an eye on what I eat and drink at the parties."

Imara sighed. "You could just not go to the parties."

"Nope. This is part of my college experience. I want to live it to the hilt. Who knows, perhaps restricted socialisation is what drove my relatives insane?"

"Are you sure that you will go nuts?"

"If I don't take precautions, yes. It is in our bloodline and could even be called a curse. We are driven to do something at all times, and if we stop, the crazy soaks in."

"Wow. That is harsh."

Bara paid the bill and slid out of the booth. "I live with my family history just like you live with yours."

Imara smiled at the point of commonality and followed Bara out of the restaurant.

Chapter Seven

The weekend flew by as Imara immersed herself in her courses and practice. She got a notice that her business course was cancelled due to lack of interest, so that left her with free Mondays. She would just have to make up the course credit elsewhere. Her email to the chancellor requesting permission to dig in the garden had been sent off, so now, she had to wait.

With her Monday free, she practiced her shape shifting and worked on forming wings and claws. The head, neck and torso structure of the bird would wait until she had her instructor watching.

You are doing very well. You haven't

had to use your emergency reversion yet. Mr. E was sitting and chewing on a very naughty claw. He had been working on it for an hour.

"I haven't transformed past the point where I could ask for help yet. I am pretty sure that when I get into that position, I am going to panic." She looked at her clawed feet poking out from beneath her bathrobe and the wings poking out of her wide kimono sleeves. Her body was urging her to complete the change, but she wasn't going to. Rushing a change was a very stupid idea.

It feels natural, does it not?

"Yeah, which is what scares me."

He looked at her with his eyes bright and tail lashing. *Why scared?*

"I have read the books about mages who got lost in their other forms, never to turn back to human. It is something to keep in mind."

You are further along than most

would be at your age.

"It doesn't make me stupid." She flicked her hands and feet back to normal, sighing as the urge to shift faded.

No, I am learning that. You have the maturity of an old soul.

She laughed. "Not likely. The lucky ones are always fresh souls, or so the legend goes."

You don't know?

She barked a laugh. "Who would tell me? There isn't a counsellor who can describe the ins and outs of being a lucky one."

Reegar appeared in her open doorway. "What would you like to know?"

Imara tightened her robe. "You know about the lucky ones?"

"Of course, I have known two. What do you need to know?" He straightened slightly. "Where are my manners; would you like tea?"

She looked down. "Sure, give me a

minute."

"You are fine. Bara is in class, and I don't care."

Imara paused. "Right. Okay. I am on my way."

She made her way down to the common area and watched Reegar prepare tea for her.

"So, what do you need to know about the lucky ones?"

She frowned. "Are they always the seventh of seven?"

"Generally. Both of the gentlemen I knew were."

"What about the child of two sevens?"

"That doesn't happen. Two seventh sons can't have a child." He tsked as if she were simple and carried over the tea tray.

She cocked her head. "What if one of the families wasn't choosy about the gender of their children and took the seventh daughter as their lucky one?"

He put a lump of sugar in her teacup and slowly poured. "The only family I know of that did that died out decades ago. It isn't an easy situation for the family and worse for the girls."

"Why?"

"She becomes an object to be traded. Her luck transfers to her children."

Imara frowned. "That doesn't seem very lucky to me."

"They are always taken care of, and all their children inherit a portion of their luck. Having lucky children becomes an extension of their luck." He put a splash of milk into her cup and slid it toward her.

"That sucks."

"Why so curious about lucky ones?"

"Luken. I want to know what I can about the birthright he inherited."

"Why?"

"Well, he is my twin."

"Oh, of course. Well, a true lucky one

gains money, power, stature, and skill. Everything they do works out in their favour." He sat back. "One of the first lucky ones I met was an investigator in the Mage Guild. He was able to bring in everyone he went after, and he was not a man to bet against at the poker table. He couldn't get drunk but always managed to get just the companion he wanted for the evening. Your brother has a bright future ahead of him."

She quirked her lips. "Good thing that I am not the lucky one in the Demiel family."

He nodded. "It is a good thing indeed. I wouldn't wish that fate on anyone."

Imara sat back and sipped at her tea. It was just the way she liked it. "No, nor would I."

They sat in silence, and she sipped her tea. So, putting it about that she was the lucky one was going to have to remain a family secret. Hopefully, the cousin who wanted Mr. E as her familiar wasn't too chatty. Luken would get enough luck from their father's side. No one would think to look at her. She could keep her luck to herself.

Shape-shifting class was all about learning to change hair and eye colour. She went through the motions with Mr. E offering colour suggestions.

"Ms. Mirrin, you are not taking this seriously."

She smiled at him and batted her lashes. "Magus Korian, I am merely having fun with colour. I thought you would appreciate seeing rainbows on this gloomy day."

He looked at her carefully. "You have excellent pigment control. You have been practicing?"

"A little, with supervising mages standing by to stop me from anything stupid."

"I am happy about the supervision, but as I am unsure as to their ability to help you, I would recommend that you keep your experimentation to this class." Korian tried to glare the message into her, and she merely stared calmly back at him.

One of the other students let out a shriek, and he hurried to his side. Their class was down to four people, and Mesook wasn't one of them. The warnings must have freaked her out. Imara didn't blame her; shape shifting was dangerous.

Reversion charms had been their first enchantment of the day. The bands would transform with them, and each held a master pattern of the mage involved. It was a nice safety net.

Imara was relieved to know that Mr. E also had her template. He was a backup drive on four feet. Reegar had made him practice resetting her until they were familiar with the process. It had been a fun Monday.

When Korian returned to her, Imara was wearing long scarlet hair and lime green eyes.

"Fine. I understand you have grasped basic transformation. Can you change your height?"

Imara rose to her feet and looked down at him from eight inches taller than her normal stature. She pointed her ears for effect. It was a pity that her clothing didn't shift with her, but that was why she was shifting and not using a glamour.

"Walk."

She made a face and took a few careful steps, wobbling at the change in balance point. With a few more steps, she had the hang of it, and soon, she was striding across the display area of the classroom with confidence.

Korian flicked his fingers, and a flash

and bang erupted in her path. Imara flinched back, and she could feel herself resuming her normal shape.

"If you were flying when that happened, you would drop out of the sky. That was a *seeming burst*. It forces reversion."

She was still facing twinges of magic running along her skin. "I am so glad you did that on purpose."

He reached out to pat her on the shoulder, but Mr. E bit his leg with a hiss and growl. Imara was startled, but she scooped her attack kitten up into her embrace.

Korian growled. "That hurt."

Imara's mind filled with images of Korian on fire and staked out and bleeding. Mr. E was so angry; he wasn't able to speak.

It wasn't the use of the reversion spell against her; it was the attempt to touch her that had set her fluffy defender off.

Korian was attracted to her, and in Mr. E's mind, he had no business pursuing that particular avenue of interaction. He was her instructor, nothing more.

"You are not to touch me in anything but an instructional manner. Patting me on the shoulder or touching me in any way that he deems inappropriate will result in my familiar taking action."

Korian's skin darkened. "Ah. Well, I suppose that is appropriate. If that little bugger bites me again, he will see my teeth."

A bone-rattling roar echoed in the room, and its origin was the tiny beast in her arms.

Imara cleared her throat. "I believe that was *challenge accepted.*"

Korian looked at the kitten who hissed and swatted back at him. "Right. I will take that under advisement."

Imara cleared her throat. "As I have demonstrated the skills for this class, may I get next week's assignment and take my familiar to calm down?"

Korian nodded sharply. "That will be for the best."

He scribbled the assignment down and handed her the document. "Out, and he had better be in a proper temper next week. Contact is part of learning to shift."

She nodded and grabbed her bag, holding her hissing and spitting familiar away from him.

If you don't calm down, I am going to have to drop that class.

He does not need to touch you, he wants to. I can smell it when he is close to you.

She grimaced and left the building. Mr. E calmed enough to climb onto her shoulder, which made carrying her books easier.

She took him home and dropped her books off, going out without speaking to him. He could have followed her, but he didn't.

Coffee seemed like a good alternative to aimlessly wandering the lanes and paths, so she headed for the shop near the edge of the campus.

After she got her order, she sat outside and picked her croissant to pieces. Dealing with lust wasn't something she was comfortable with, especially when it was someone who was alive. She had dropped Mr. E off because she didn't need his voice in her head while she figured out what she wanted to do.

Imara was into her second cup of coffee when a black SUV pulled up and disgorged three XIA agents. She recognized one of them immediately. To her consternation, he smiled and walked over.

"Imara, funny meeting you here."

"Hi, Argus. I didn't know that the XIA engaged in enforcement on campus." She wrapped her hands around her mug and tried to look casual while her heart was hammering in her chest.

A vampire wearing shades and a baseball hat came up next to the griffin, and a fey glided up on his left. The smooth tones of the elf were unforgettable. "Argus, won't you introduce us to your friend?"

She really didn't think she wanted to know those guys. The vampire looked like he ate horseshoes for breakfast, and the elf had enough muscle to pull out trees with his pinky. They made Argus look lithe in comparison, and his forearm was nearly as wide as her thigh.

They were all wearing black on black, the shirts tailored but snug. The XIA badge was carefully picked out in black and bronze with the logo of their particular extranatural affiliation underneath.

Argus scowled but remembered his manners. "Ivar, Lio, this is my ethics classmate, Imara Mirrin. Imara, these are the assholes I work with."

She grinned. "Pleased to meet you. Are you just passing through?"

"We had some appointments with the dean of students and some witnesses."

The men moved forward and took the empty seats around her table. The metal and wood creaked in protest.

Argus gave Ivar a glare, and the vampire got to his feet and lumbered inside.

Lio leaned forward. "So, Argus turns to jelly whenever he mentions taking the class. I am guessing you are the cause?"

She blinked. "I have no idea about that."

The fey had silvery features in skin so pale it was nearly warm moonlight. The delicate skin was stretched over wide musculature in a most disconcerting way. She didn't know much about fey, but he wasn't a proper elf.

He snorted indelicately and then made a muffled sound as Argus clapped a hand over his mouth.

"Ignore him, Imara, he is just hungry. We aren't normally up and about at this time of day, but the college insisted."

"So, you are here because of the magic drain? Why didn't they just send the guild?" Imara sipped at her coffee.

"The women affected have no magic. Therefore, they don't fall under the guild's protection." Argus scowled, releasing Lio's face when Ivar showed up with a tray full of coffees.

Ivar smiled at her, not showing his fangs. "I didn't know what you were drinking, so I got a selection."

The stack of pastries was the first casualty as Lio dug in.

"You didn't have to get me anything, but thank you."

She picked a cup labelled two cream and two sugar. Argus grinned and grabbed his own, then frowned. "Speaking of women under attack, why are you here alone? Where is your familiar?”

The fey was fascinated. “You have a familiar?”

She smirked. “Yeah. He bit my shape-shifting instructor, so now, I have to figure out a way to deal with that.”

Argus beamed. “You are learning to shape shift?”

She grimaced as Ivar snickered. “Yes.”

Lio asked, “What form have you chosen? Are you going to match your familiar?”

She let out a snort. “No. I have picked something a little bigger.”

Argus filled his partners in. “Her familiar is a kitten.”

The two agents chortled and drank their coffee while Argus leaned toward her. “What did you choose as your beast?”

She blushed. “You are going to read something into it.”

He looked surprised. "I won't."

"Griffin vulture."

By the hoots of hilarity that her companions were letting out and the smug look in Argus's eyes, they had read something into it.

Chapter Eight

"I am strongly suggesting that you don't go out alone until the magic drain is found," Argus stated it at her door. "Keep your familiar with you when you are on campus."

"I like to have time alone. I am used to it."

"Tough. Being twitchy is no reason to be stupid. He has power, let him protect you."

She cackled. "Right, like he protected me from my creepy shifting instructor."

His face went from lecturing to steel. "What?"

"Mr. E says that the teacher smells like lust when he is around me, so when the teacher approached me, Mr. E attacked. It was a cute and fuzzy attack, but he still bit him."

She had never seen a growl pass over someone's features before. Muscles moved under the skin, and his lip curled.

"Uh, right. So, I was out on my own trying to figure out a plan of attack, so to speak."

"He tried to touch you?"

"Just pat my shoulder, but then, he said that shifting requires a lot of contact and that didn't seem right when he was instructing the rest of the class by pointing and using an illustration."

A full-body shudder went through Argus. "When is your next class?"

"Monday morning. I have a week to refine my approach." She smiled. "Thanks for the coffee. It was interesting to meet Lio and Ivar."

He chuckled. "They were enchanted

by you."

"Yes, it was nice when Ivar mentioned that I was younger than his wallet." She wrinkled her nose. "I promise to use the buddy system around campus."

"Good. See you in class tomorrow." He bowed slightly and left.

She exhaled slowly and watched him go. *Too old for you, too old for you, too old for you.* Her own mind beat her with the truth.

She leaned out to look around the corner of the building as he stepped into his vehicle. The flex of his muscles could be discerned, even from her distance. She exhaled slowly again and headed inside.

Mr. E ran up to her and climbed her leg, heading up to his perch on her shoulder. *I am sorry I lost my temper... Why do you smell like griffin?*

Argus and his team have been assigned to the investigation here at the college. They had a meeting with the dean and stopped for coffee. I was at the coffee shop, trying to figure out how to deal with Korian.

An amused chuckle ran through her thoughts; this time it wasn't her. *Did you let Argus know about Korian?*

Yes.

Oh... this is going to be fun to watch.

She didn't know what he meant by that, but she tried to think positive.

Argus was waiting in the hall when she arrived for the ethics class, and he smiled in greeting. They were the only ones there, and she was fifteen minutes early. She had no idea how long he had been waiting.

The snickering of her familiar was getting annoying.

The lecture was long, but the teaching assistant had their assignments graded and handed back by the end of the class.

Imara sighed in relief. Getting ninety percent or higher was part of her business plan. If her grades were high enough, she would get an equivalence pass on certain courses. It was part of her accelerated graduation plan.

She glanced at Argus's paper and smiled. An eighty-six was nothing to sneeze at.

She folded her graded paper and tucked it into the envelope at the back of her binder.

"You are very meticulous when it comes to your notes," Argus commented as they got up after the lecture.

"Yes. I was once accused of cheating when I was younger, so now I keep track of each and every bit of information I get."

"Did you cheat?" He nudged her with his elbow.

"Of course not. I made an intuitive leap that made my teacher look bad. It was not a great moment for Mrs. Heckle's third-grade history class." She shook her head ruefully. "After that, I kept all my notes, tests, and reports."

"Wow. Third grade, huh?"

"Yeah. I am hardcore now."

Mr. E was purring happily at their banter.

"May I escort you to your home?"

She shook her head. "No, I am heading off for lunch."

He paused and asked politely, "May I join you?"

"You are going to look a bit odd in the cafeteria."

"We could go off campus. There is a noodle place a few miles away."

She made a face. "Do you mind if I work on the assignment?"

"No. That was my plan as well."

"Excellent. Do you want to drive, or shall I?" She grinned.

"My vehicle is nearby."

"Oh, good. Mine is parked in hell's half acre. Lead the way."

Argus grinned and took point.

Imara was face deep in noodles with Mr. E happily experiencing sushi for the first time when Argus dropped a conversational bomb.

"I would like permission to court you when your studies are over."

She finished her slurp on a cough. Her voice was a hoarse squeak. "What?"

Argus was looking at her earnestly. "I would like permission to court you when you have finished college and settled in your career."

"Um... are you putting dibs on me?" She stared at him in consternation while the snickering from her familiar was nearly audible.

He cocked his head. "Something like that. I know you do not have time for a relationship, nor do I wish to be a distraction for you while you are studying."

"That is very thoughtful. You would be waiting for three years."

He shrugged. "Time isn't a problem, and I notice that you did not say no."

Her skin flushed. "Ah, yeah. That. Well, I didn't say no. That's true."

He smiled; his metallic eyes sparkled. "I will take that as your offer to consider it."

"You are happy with that?"

"Delighted."

Mr. E got up, stretched and wandered over to Argus, looking him up and down. The diabolical kitten reached into Argus's bowl and caught a pawful of noodles and chicken.

Argus didn't do anything as the kitten scarfed down the stolen goods.

What are you doing, you little maniac?

Testing your would-be mate. He is going to have to get used to me one way or another.

That can be accomplished without your digging in his food. I would have given you some of mine if you had asked.

This is more fun. I am enjoying teasing a large predator with you here to defend me.

That is it.

She leaned forward and scooped the black, fluffy serial killer up and spanked him, setting him back at his plate.

Argus grinned. "I bet he didn't like that."

I didn't even feel it. This body is all bounce and fluff. He flicked his tail in the air. *And you hit like a girl.*

She chuckled. "He is getting over it. So, how long have you been partnered with Lio and Ivar? Are all XIA agents so huge?"

"We are heavy hitters. We get called in for extranaturals who are rampaging or overpowering. Lots of trolls." He smiled.

"I have never met a troll." She slurped at her noodles then put a small portion in front of Mr. E with a selection of carrots and chicken. He didn't say anything, but purring commenced.

"Well, you sort of have. Lio is half troll, half elf."

She whistled softly. "That explains a lot. What about Ivar?"

Argus chuckled. "I think he ate a troll and it got stuck."

She giggled at the mental image and then sobered. "If we put off courtship for years, what are we in the meantime?"

"Friends? Companions? Classmates? If I get desperate, study buddies?"

She laughed. "Do I get to pick?"

"Of course."

"Friends then. Platonic and casual friends who can study together if you get desperate."

He grinned. "I will take you up on that if your familiar doesn't mind."

The low rumbling purr coming from the tiny body was answer enough.

Argus straightened and asked, "So, what did you get for answer three?"

She smiled and returned to her soup. "No action shall be taken against the powerless unless they have been armed by a mage."

"Ah, right. Okay... on to question seven."

She enjoyed studying with him and having endless cups of tea appearing while the old cups were whisked away. None of the staff even raised a brow at Mr. E.

Homework had never been so entertaining with a side of flirting. It was going to be a long few years.

Chapter Nine

$\mathcal{H}$aving members of the XIA roaming the campus at night cut down on the escalating incidences of draining, but it was the effect of Argus visiting her shifting class that made Imara feel safe.

Magus Korian had been star struck at a genuine mythical shifter sitting in on his class.

Imara had gotten down to business and fully shifted into her vulture. Argus had her extend her wings, and he had been very businesslike about telling her what parts of her form she needed to alter for flight.

Korian was hovering in the background, but with an actual flying shifter helping her with her scale, he didn't have anything to offer.

"Okay, now beat your wings." Argus smiled.

She flapped twice, and to her shock, her feet lifted off the ground. She was so surprised that she landed heavily on her tail feathers.

"It is fine. Everybody lands on their butt now and then. Come on; I will help you up, and you can glide to a tremendous landing on your stomach."

Before she could do more than shriek in panic and flap her wings, he scooped her up, and her claws were digging into his forearm.

With the rest of the class watching, he walked to the back of the auditorium, and her vision focused on the stage and the tempting prey of the small, black kitten.

She got her balance and focused, hearing the taunt from below. *Bring it on, baldy.*

She didn't shriek, didn't make a sound as she launched from her perch and glided toward her prey.

She hit him hard. The sound was a meaty thud, but instead of perching on him, she used her momentum to carry him up and into the rafters.

Baldy? Really?

Oh, you heard that? I mean you are a lovely example of vulture nobility.

She perched and let him slip out of her claws. If he weren't a creature of magic, he would have been crushed when she snagged him.

She sat for a moment and watched the faces turned toward her. Only Argus was watching with a smile on his face.

Imara shook her head, looked at Mr. E and asked, *So, how do you feel about landing?*

He grumbled but got into a position where she could grab him.

She walked sideways, grabbed him, spread her wings, and began to flex and flap, lowering them at a predictable pace. She released her familiar a few feet from the ground and then dropped to the wooden floor.

Imara sat and breathed heavily as she took her human form again. The charm she was wearing generated her robe, and she sat on her ass and wiggled her toes in front of the class. "Well, that was fun."

Korian was staring at her, blinking in shock. "You... you made a complete transformation with only two classes."

Argus wandered up to her and helped her to her feet. She smiled brightly. "I had some coaching."

Korian nodded, and he shrugged. "Well, you have proved proficiency. You get the class credit."

"What?"

"The course aim was to achieve a secondary form that was functional and biologically sound. You flew, landed and flew again. That gets you a pass."

"Oh. Right. Well, thanks. I will just get changed and leave."

"That would be best. The other students still have a lot to learn."

"Oh. What about the final exam?"

"You just did it." Korian smiled and took a step toward her, trying to reach out to her.

Argus moved, and Korian froze, retreating as he stared at the XIA agent.

"Right, well, I will file your passing grade with the college. You should receive a confirmation within the hour."

"Thank you, Magus Korian. It was an informative class."

She scooped up Mr. E and stroked him lightly as she walked to where she had left her day clothing. She pulled her panties and jeans on under her robe, turned her back and put on her bra before yanking her shirt on over her head.

Mr. E was watching to make sure that no one was peeping at more than her back for a few seconds. Once she was dressed, she pulled on her shoes and grabbed her bag and books with Mr. E taking up his accustomed perch on her shoulder.

Argus looked at her. "Would you like to get lunch?"

Her stomach churned and growled. She blushed. "How did you know?"

"Shifting shape always takes a toll."

"I want to change clothing first. I think I have my shirt on backward, and I have put on enough of a show for the day."

"Lead the way." He grinned.

She took off with a long stride, and he kept up with her as she made her way across the campus. Her body was energized, and she needed to use that energy or scream.

When they arrived at Reegar Hall, she invited him into the common room. "Wait here, and I will be right back."

Reegar looked up in surprise from the easy chair where he was reading his favourite spell book. "You are leaving him here?"

She smiled. "Just for a minute. I am just going to change clothing, and we will be on our way. Don't do anything weird while I am gone."

Argus glanced her way. "Which one of us are you talking to?"

"Both." She headed up the stairs and made a beeline for her room. Her bag thudded on the floor, and she sent her shirt and Mr. E flying, noting that it was inside out and he was excellent at landing on the bed. Her twisted bra was banished to the hamper, and her jeans followed.

She was dressed in a properly behaving bra, sweatshirt, and fresh jeans in under two minutes. She brushed her hair out and flipped it behind her, extended her arm to Mr. E, and her familiar was back in place on her shoulders when she finished tying her sneakers.

"Ready to go?"

Your purse.

"Thank you. You are an excellent familiar."

I know it.

She pried her purse out of her backpack and checked it quickly. There were money, keys, and her identification readily visible next to her phone, so she was good to go.

"Huh. I have a message."

She woke up her phone and listened to the message. She had clearance to dig up the soil she needed. She just had to make an appointment to be accompanied by a member of the chancellor's household.

As she walked down the stairs, she

made the call.

Reegar and Argus were sitting and appeared involved in deep conversation.

With her appointment looming, she grabbed some plastic bags, a knife, and a spoon. They would help her do what she needed to do.

"So, what were you and Reegar discussing?"

Argus drove them off campus and out to the town again. "Just his enjoyment of you as a tenant. You seem enthusiastic about something. Good news?"

"Yeah, I get to go digging to get some soil that will hopefully let me pass my herbology course."

He blinked. "You have to find your own dirt?"

"Yeah. It is for the final exam, but plants take time. I have to get the plants under way as soon as possible, but the chancellor's office delayed in getting back to me."

"You need fancy dirt?" He glanced at her.

"I need magical dirt. I am pinning my hopes on the slightly risqué memoire of a previous student."

"Really?"

"Yeah, I am trusting my own magic and hoping for the best." Her stomach snarled again.

He chuckled. "Hang in there. We will be there in a moment."

"Where are we going?"

"Barbeque. You have just had your first shift, you need meat. Mage or not, your body has just had a shock."

He pulled his blue SUV into a parking lot and found a spot. The moment that the car settled he was around the vehicle and had her door open.

"Um, I thought we were pausing the idea of courtship for a few years."

He took her hand in his. "Just helping you out of the car, buddy."

She rolled her eyes while Mr. E snickered.

"Oh, can he come in?"

"Yes. This is a shifter-friendly estab-
lishment. The occasional ball of fur
doesn't even faze folks."

The car door shut behind her, and he
led her into the restaurant with his fingers woven with hers. It was more than
the assistance of a friend, but she didn't
want to fuss.

The air in the parking lot was full of
the scent of barbeque, so Imara walked
faster. Once inside, the server was
friendly, told Mr. E what a pretty boy he
was and took them to a table.

"Huh, this really is familiar friendly."

"Well, the college is ten minutes
away. He probably isn't even the only
one in here today."

She ordered a soda and water, he settled for green tea.

The menus were bursting with meat,

but before she could make up her mind, Argus snagged her menu from her and shook his head. "Trust me on this. I will pick what you need. The first shift meal needs to be special."

Imara drummed her fingertips on the table. "Special?"

"Oh, yes. Just a moment."

He left the table, and she was sitting there with Mr. E still basking in the comment of the hostess.

A moment later, Argus reappeared and took his seat with a smile on his lips. "It will just be a moment."

It was two minutes of stomach churning sounds before a server arrived and slid moist towelettes down before she delivered some riblets covered in sauce.

She grinned. "The rest will be out in a few minutes."

Imara tore open the wipe and grabbed a riblet. To her amusement, the server brought a small plate of shredded pork for Mr. E. He happily launched himself to the table while the ladies squealed and cooed at him while they went about their rounds.

Perhaps being cute isn't too bad.

Imara was halfway through the small tidbits of pork on bone when he spoke. *See? I told you so.*

Argus sipped at his tea. "Has that taken the edge off?"

Her stomach rumbled again. "A little bit. I no longer feel hollow."

"You had a mass dispersal. You are not going to feel great for a couple of days, and you will need massive meals. It is my honour to provide you with your first shift meal." Argus said the words with solemn formality.

"I thank you for the upcoming meal; now, please join me before I eat everything." She looked at the half dozen bits left on the plate, the clean bones stacked neatly beside them.

Argus picked up a wet nap and slowly cleaned his hands. He picked up one of the little bits and raised it to his lips.

The server arrived with a platter for two and set it firmly in front of Imara. Argus had a salad.

She looked at him over the display of ambrosia to her senses. "You have to be joking."

"No. You need this."

"Have some."

He grinned. "Thank you. It is up to you to share your kill, or in this case, your chicken and ribs."

"But..." she gave him an arch look. "The brisket is mine."

He inclined his head in acceptance, and the feeding frenzy began.

Chapter Ten

"**W**hy aren't I full?" She looked down at her hands, still stained from the sauce after the two double platters. The soap in the bathroom wasn't up to the task.

"You lost molecular density. You lost mass to take your form, and when you shifted back, you didn't regain all of that mass. Basically, you forgot where you parked it. Your instructor should have shown you how to do it."

"I am not sure that he knows. He wanted us all to pick a shape that had nearly the same mass as our human bodies. I had to pick the one that called to me, but the others were pretty much matching their human forms."

"You did very well. Controlling the transformation is important. If you like, I can give you some instruction so that you can gain proficiency."

"That would be nice. Thanks again for the meal."

"First shift is a rite of passage amongst shape shifters. It is our only magic, so we celebrate it."

She smiled. "Yeah, I am getting that. Could you drop us at the chancellor's residence?"

"Certainly. Would you like help to dig?"

"I won't need help, but I wouldn't mind the company."

He grinned.

"Wait, don't you have to work this evening?" She bit her lip, worried that she was monopolizing his time.

"I don't need as much sleep as you do. I will be fine and up to class tomorrow."

He smiled and turned with practiced ease through the twisting streets of the campus.

The chancellor's residence was nearly as old as the college and had ivy covering the exterior.

"Wow. This is neat."

"Haven't you been here before?"

Imara shook her head. "Nope. I have met the chancellor a few times, but I haven't been to the residence."

He parked in a gravelled lot, and they left the vehicle together, walking up the path to the ancient home.

Before they could knock, the door opened, and a young man stood in the opening. "Imara Mirrin?"

"Yes."

"I am Dresden Deepford-Smythe, the chancellor's assistant. I will take you to the gardens."

She sighed at facing one of her cousins. "Thank you."

The assistant emerged from the house and walked them around the building to the gated gardens. This wasn't a standard gate. The garden was guarded by a seven-foot stone wall that radiated magic. Dresden opened the gate for them and nodded. "You have two hours until the garden ejects you. I hope you find what you are looking for."

Imara nodded and stepped into the gardens, looking past the glowing and lush flowers and seeking the pear tree.

"What are we looking for?"

"A pear tree. I am looking for a pear tree."

As she walked, she dug blindly into her purse until she found the test strips.

Argus looked at the vial with interest. "What is that?"

"Magic detector. It hasn't had a field test yet, but I thought it might help."

She held the tweezers and flipped open the vial, selecting one out of the fifty little strips. She walked toward the large orchard section of the gardens and let one of the strips fall.

There was a minor flash on the ground, and Imara grinned. "Excellent."

"What did that prove?"

"There is magic. If it isn't magical, nothing happens."

He nodded. "Right. Can your familiar help?"

"I don't know. Mr. E, can you find the pear tree?"

He snuffled against her neck. *Fourth tree, two rows down. It was there when I went to school.*

She gestured, and they followed the direction of her tiny food-coma'd companion.

The pear tree was moving, but there was no wind. It was a good sign.

"I am going to drop another strip. You might want to guard your eyes."

She let one tiny piece flutter to the

root of the pear tree. The flash of light nearly blinded her. "Found it."

Argus watched her cap the vial. "Where did you get those?"

"I made them for this purpose. I can dig here." She dropped to her knees and took out her bags, knife, and spoon. Mr. E kept his balance neatly.

"What are you doing?"

"I don't want to disrupt the appearance of the gardens, so I thought I would slice up the sod and peel it back before I dig out the soil."

"May I speed up the process?"

"As long as you keep the garden neat."

He extended his hand, shifted it to display large claws, and he sliced the grass in a one-foot cube that he carefully pried upward and set aside.

"There you go. Get spooning."

"Thanks for that." She took her spoon and the bags and collected a few pounds of soil. When she was done and the bags were sealed, she replaced the sod cut and tapped it down. It sank a bit but was otherwise fine.

As Imara stared, the soil filled up again and the turf fused into a pristine condition. "That was weird."

He chuckled. "Yes, it was. Shall we go?"

She nodded, and they followed the path they had taken through the gardens. When they stepped through the gate, it slammed shut behind them.

Imara jumped, and Argus turned slowly. "I am guessing our time was up."

She nodded. "That seems like a safe assumption. Well, thank you for the meal and the ride back."

He gave her a look. "I am escorting you back to your hall."

She wrinkled her nose. "Thank you. That is very thoughtful."

They walked back to his car, and she

carefully kept the bags of soil on her lap.

"So, why do you need magical soil?"

"Herbology class. To make potions, you need herbs, and magical herbs make the potions more effective. Magical soil helps make magical herbs, and that increases the effect of the potions."

"Sensible. What exactly do those strips that you used do?"

"They detect magic. The stronger the magic, the more violent the reaction apparently." She got the vial out and used the tweezers to remove the strip. She put it on the dashboard, and nothing happened.

"Nothing is happening."

"Well, unless you enchanted this car, nothing would happen. However, if I touch it or you touch it, it would flare."

She carefully closed the container and attached the tweezer to the band.

The little piece of paper sat on the dashboard as he drove her back to Reegar Hall.

When they were parked again, she reached out and touched the strip with the tip of her finger.

"Damn! I should not have been watching that." She covered her eyes with her free hand. Sparks and shadowed rainbows were in her vision for several seconds.

"Have you tested your familiar?" Argus's voice was amused.

"No. I don't want to go blind." She muttered it, and Mr. E silently snickered.

She blinked and her vision stabilized. "Whew. That is better."

"Didn't you test it on yourself?"

"Nope. I know I am magical. I know you are magical. I sure as hell know that Mr. E isn't natural. That left your car."

He left the car and walked around to open her door for her. The first time it was weird; now, she just let him do it.

She gathered her bags, checked Mr. E, and swung her legs out of the vehicle before she realized she was still buckled. A bit of muttering and some fumbling later, she hopped to the ground and glanced at his grinning countenance. "You didn't see anything."

"Madam, I am an XIA agent, I am trained to see everything." He bowed, and they walked from the guest parking, across the quad, and over to Reegar Hall.

He was made of curiosity. "Where do you get the herbs that you plant?"

"I have already picked them from fields and public gardens around the college. They are at the hall, waiting for a proper receptacle."

"The building is very cold from the outside. Are you happy there?"

She chuckled. "I love it. There are only two of us there so far. I know that Reegar is being pressured to take more students on, so I am enjoying it while it lasts."

"Magus Reegar is a little strange. He doesn't smell like anything."

She chuckled. "That is because he isn't alive. He is a spectre."

"He was holding a book."

She blushed, "Yeah, remember when I told you that I turbocharged spectres? I can also make them solid with enough exposure."

"Can he wander freely?"

"No, he is tethered to his building, or within fifty feet of it, just like any spectre."

"Ah. He seemed so alive."

"He is living consciousness. He has the same hopes, dreams, and desires that he did when he was alive. His soul has probably been recycled already."

"Recycled... you mean reincarnated?"

"Same thing." She hugged the bags of dirt to her chest.

"So, there are two of him?"

"No. The soul has a body. Reegar's spectre is forever the same age with different experiences. He loves the same man he loved when alive and is lucky enough to have his lover be practically immortal."

"They have seen each other?"

"A few times. It is so sweet. With the internet, it is a whole new take on their relationship."

They approached the hall, and he walked her right to the door.

"Would you like to come in and discuss his afterlife with him?"

He chuckled. "No. I will see you in class tomorrow. Congratulations on your first shift, my friend."

He leaned in and kissed her cheek, turned, and walked away.

Her heart was pounding in her chest, and Mr. E was laughing uproariously in her mind.

She got into the building, went to her room, and dumped Mr. E on the bed. He lifted his hind leg and groomed his toes, looking at her with direct eye contact.

You are never going to make it three years.

She only needed two scoops of the soil, and the herbs stretched, flourished, and glowed.

"Damn. What am I going to do with the rest of this?"

Store it. That kind of power isn't something that you should waste.

"Right."

She got a canister and slipped the two closed bags of soil into it, marking it carefully with the words, *Enchanted dirt—do not touch.*

Why aren't you out with Bara tonight?

"I didn't want to. I wanted to get the planting done, just in case the soil didn't work."

You knew it would.

"I wasn't sure. I am never sure. Using luck to figure stuff out isn't reliable. Sometimes it leads me down a path that will benefit me in the long term but sucks in the short term."

So, you were worried about failing your herbology course?

"I am worried about turning myself into a large squid."

Ah. Well, you might need to see a therapist.

She grinned and picked him up, snuggling her face into his fur. "Why get a therapist when I have you?"

He squirmed before settling and purring. *I despise being a slave to my baser urges. Scratch under my chin.*

She grinned and did as her familiar requested. With the lab tidied up, she headed up to her room for a well-earned rest. It had been a very full day.

Her dream of playing bongos turned into the sound of someone pounding on her door.

"Imara! Wake up!" A hand shook her shoulder.

She jerked awake, and her lights were on with Reegar staring at her with a frantic expression. "What? What's wrong?"

"Bara. Bara is the latest victim. She's downstairs."

"Shit." She got out of bed and jerked on her robe. Mr. E ran ahead of her as she stumbled down the steps.

Bara was sitting in the common space, tears running down her cheeks. Ivar and Lio were trying to question her while Argus was speaking with someone on the phone.

Imara stepped in, close enough to hear what Bara was saying but far enough to let the XIA agents do their jobs.

"I drank a soda, and then the world got blurry. I woke up, and I felt hollow." Bara wiped at her tears, her bandaged fingers moving with short jerks.

Imara wanted to do something, so she did. She rushed to the lab and pulled the ingredients for the reversion charm together. It was all she could think to do.

"Mr. E, can you grab one of Bara's bandages, preferably one that has touched a burst blister?"

I can burst it. Back in a minute.

In a handful of heartbeats, she heard a shout of confusion and a shriek of surprise.

Mr. E had done an excellent job. He brought three bandages in, and two of them were stained with white cells and blood.

She pressed the stained gauze into the paste she had prepared, and she poured magic into it, using as many time-bending chants as she could.

The mess in the bowl hardened into a scarlet jewel. She got some tongs and picked up the charm. "Stand back."

Mr. E stayed out of her way as she walked to the common room. Lio must have read her expression because he pulled Ivar away from Bara.

"Hold out your hands."

Bara sniffled and extended her hands, catching the charm in her palms.

"Repeat after me. Chrono-Key-Amber."

"Chrono-Key-Amber." Bara leaned forward, and the charm started to glow. "What is it doing?"

"It is resetting you by two hours. Your body will be like it was two hours ago. I don't know how long it will last, but you can repeat the call on the charm when it wears off, just don't drop the charm." Imara knelt in front of her, exhausted.

"How did you..." Bara trailed off and

smiled, opening her hand and conjuring a ball of light.

"Shape-shifting reversion charm. I used your broken blister to reset you. It was all I could think of."

Mr. E brushed up against her and purred; she could feel him trying to support her with his tiny body.

Reegar was explaining what had taken place to the XIA agents, but Imara didn't care. She passed out where she was.

Chapter Eleven

Three worried faces were staring at her when she woke, and Mr. E was on her head.

"Hey, agents, why the worried faces?" She sat up, and Mr. E transferred to her lap.

Argus crouched next to her. "You fainted."

"I did not faint. I surrendered to exhaustion. There is a difference."

Bara was curled up in the chair, her chest moving evenly.

Reegar brought her a cup of tea. "Here you go."

"Thank you, Magus."

"That was inspired spell work. Where

did you find the time charm?"

"Eberhart's Enchantments. It was theoretical. I am glad it seems to work."

Reegar walked toward the library and came back a few minutes later with the book in his hands. "Show me."

She set the teacup and saucer down and flipped rapidly through the pages until she got to the one she was looking for.

"Here it is." Imara handed the book back to him.

He took the book and frowned. "You should not have been able to do this."

"Why?"

"It is an immortality spell."

She looked over at Bara and then to the XIA agents who looked a little surprised. "Um, sorry?"

"Don't be sorry, but this shouldn't work."

"I guess I got lucky that it did." She smiled tightly and finished the tea.

"Yes, that would describe it. Bara is doing well. The charm you gave her is keeping her magic flowing, but we need to know who took it."

She looked to the XIA. "Can any of you track magic?"

They shook their heads.

I can.

She looked at Mr. E. "Seriously?"

Of course. Would you like me to track Bara?

"Let me get dressed." She stood, and Argus moved to block her.

"Where do you think you are going?"

"Mr. E says he can track Bara's magic. He knows her well and knows me, so he won't be thrown by my scent in the spell."

"He can lead us."

"No, he can't. He is my familiar; he can only communicate with me." She glared into his metallic eyes. "Out of my way, buddy."

He stepped aside.

She ran back to her room, dropped her robe and pajamas and then pulled on her jeans and a t-shirt. Underwear wasn't necessary, she was on a mission in the middle of the night.

She yanked on her sneakers and headed downstairs. "Mr. E, lead the way."

Argus grabbed her arm. "You can come with, but let us go first."

"You can come with me. You won't be able to find Mr. E if he hits the shadows."

He paused, Lio nodded. "Right. Stay with at least one of us."

Mr. E yowled and pawed at the door.

"Agreed. Let's go." She nodded, and Ivar opened the door.

They sprinted after the tiny shadow as he sniffed out the magic trail.

Argus stayed next to her, and he muttered, "This is where she was found."

Mr. E circled the area several times and then yowled again. *I have it!*

The small bundle of fluff streaked off away from the shadowed space between buildings and ran into the open door of the house where the party had just been held.

Students were holed up in every corner of the rooms. Couples were making out, and some exhausted and disappointed singles were cleaning up with unsteady motions.

Mr. E was feeding her his senses, and he tuned out the smells of sweat, sex, and vomit. He was on the trail of magic.

They worked their way into the centre of the building where the ancient structure hosted a ballroom. The small bundle of fluff made a beeline toward the bar, and he crouched on the ground, growling with his tail lashing.

Lio and Ivar halted and waited for her to tell them what was going on.

She made eye contact with the woman behind the bar that was loaded with non-alcoholic drinks.

"It's her. She has Bara's magic."

As she spoke, the woman decided to act. She jumped over the bar and ran.

The agents were after the fleeing in a moment, and Imara collected Mr. E. "You did well, little buddy."

Thank you. She should not have messed with Bara. If the agents weren't here, I would have dealt with her.

"I am glad you didn't have to. Let's get back home." She cuddled him and made her way back through the detritus of the party and into the night air.

The path to Reegar Hall was longer than it had seemed on the way out. She walked past a few spectres and nodded to them politely. It was nice when they nodded back.

Watch out! There is—

She was hit hard in the side and

knocked to the ground, sending Mr. E flying. The grass was crushed as she skidded to a halt and the scent of soil was in her nose.

She turned, and the bartender was standing above her, her chest heaving and fists clenched. "It was perfect, bitch. Everyone was looking at the men."

Imara tried to get to her feet, but the woman kicked her in the chest.

"The drink would have made this easier, but you have enough to keep me strong enough to start over."

Imara saw tendrils of darkness coming toward her and inhaled sharply just as a low growl came from her left.

Acid green light flared, and a roar distracted Imara's attacker. Imara rolled rapidly to the side and got to her feet in time to see a giant panther tackle the woman and crush her throat in his jaws. The cat held her and shook her hard. The snap of her neck was horribly audible.

The cat let her go and turned to Imara, pacing toward her, his red eyes blazing and the green flames snapping around his silky black body. She leaned back, and he kept advancing, shifting into his kitten form and rubbing against her leg.

She whispered, "I didn't know you could do that."

I didn't either. None of my other forms had this option, but she was going to kill you, and my body transformed.

"I suppose that is a good thing."

You are alive. It is a very good thing.

The XIA agents appeared at the far end of the green space, running toward them intently.

She held tightly to Mr. E and watched Argus and the others as they slowed and walked carefully toward the body.

Argus asked, "What happened?"

"She knocked me down, kicked me and was going to do whatever she did to Bara, only without the sedation."

"What happened?"

She buried her fingers in Mr. E's fur. "My familiar stopped her."

Lio looked surprised. "Your kitten?"

"He's not a kitten. He's an energy projection with the soul of an ancient magus. He's registered if that is what you are worried about." She bit her lip.

Ivar was kneeling next to the body. "She's very dead. Her throat is crushed."

Argus frowned. "Go to the hall. We will be there when we have taken care of the body."

Lio nodded. "I will call it in."

She bobbed her head and walked briskly across the grass and toward Reegar Hall.

Magus Reegar met her at the door and ushered her inside. He settled her on the couch in the common room, covered her shoulders in a blanket and got her another cup of tea.

You can let me go now.

She sighed and relaxed her grip. *I just wanted to hold you for a bit. I don't think I have ever been that scared.*

In that case, scratch my belly.

Imara sighed in relief and scratched his tummy. He curled in her arms, and she kept petting him while the vision of him killing her attacker rang in her mind.

"Bara's normal magic returned ten minutes ago. I took the charm from her and put it in the lab. She's gone to bed."

"Good. We found the culprit, and she's dead now."

"It was a woman?"

"It was. Black energy. I haven't seen anything like it." She thought about it. "I have seen a soul eater before, but its magic was more of a grey wisp."

"Black? Let me consult the library."

She looked at the stacks of books and got to her feet. "Maybe I can help."

"If it keeps you busy. You are in shock."

"Yeah, I would agree with that." She walked into the library and ran her hand over the ancient books on the shelves, letting her fingertips caress the spines.

She had made it through two-thirds of the books when her fingers tingled. "Got one."

"Ah, *Definitions of Power*. That is likely."

They took the book to the study table and opened it. She kept petting Mr. E as he purred and her blood pressure gradually reached normal levels.

The pages of the book turned one after another with a wide collection of information on power signatures and focuses. An illustration of black tendrils was suddenly front and centre.

"That's it."

Reegar looked at it and read aloud. "'Magus inversion. A mage who has suffered a severe psychic injury can begin to consume the magic of others in order to function normally.' It appears to be a nice word for psychic vampire."

A female voice spoke behind them. "There is no nice word for it."

Imara turned and saw the chancellor. "Magus Deepford-Smythe. I would say good evening, but it really isn't."

"No. I need to check your mind, Imara. I just have to confirm that you weren't the cause of the death. I need to see her last moments."

Imara nodded. "Go ahead."

Soft touches at her temples and she saw the evening on fast forward. When the replay was over, her mother slowly broke contact. "So, you were defended by your familiar. That is within the bounds of self-defense. I will report it to the guild, but they may still want to question you. It is fine. You didn't do anything wrong."

"Thanks. It is good to hear it."

Mr. E was still purring in her arms.

Her mother looked at her familiar and inclined her head. "Thank you for watching over my daughter."

Mr. E squirmed until he was sitting properly in Imara's arm, and he nodded his head formally.

Tell her that I accept her thanks and that you are worthy of protection.

"Uh, he says that he accepts your thanks." She smiled tightly.

Mr. E dug his claws into her arm.

"And that I am worthy of protection. Though he doesn't seem to think so right now." She flexed her arm and set him on the table.

Mirrin made a hesitant move toward her and then hugged her. "I am relieved you are all right."

"Thank you. Aside from it being your

job, I am glad you are here. I needed a hug."

Reegar chuckled. "I would have offered it, but I have never been good at commiseration."

Mr. E licked his front foot and started washing his face. *I am an excellent soothing companion.*

Yes, you are, but there is nothing like a mother's hug.

He cleaned his fur, and her mother released her. Mirrin smiled. "I will have Luken check on you this afternoon."

"That will be fine. I have an ethics class in the morning."

"Oh, Imara. Do you think you should? You have had a shock."

"My instructor is a douchebag, so I don't want to give him an excuse for a bad grade. I will go even if I take a nap during the lecture."

Argus came in and walked up to her, ignoring the chancellor. "Imara, are you all right?"

"I am fine, just a little shaken. Bara has regained her power, but I don't know what the situation with the others is."

Mirrin looked between them. "Have you met?"

Imara began blushing. "Ah, yes. We have. We share an ethics course and have gone to coffee and lunch a few times. He also coached me for my shifter class. We're friends."

Argus smirked as she babbled. "We have agreed to a delayed courtship."

Her mother's mouth opened and closed in surprise. "I see. I believe I am going to have to speak with your superiors to get a gauge of your character."

"Chancellor?" Argus was confused.

Imara decided to explain while Reegar was trying not to laugh. "She is my mother."

He stared at both of them in turn, and

then, his lips quirked. "Well, that explains the similarities."

Imara sighed and picked up her familiar again. "I am a little tired, and the chancellor has confirmed my version of events so if you don't mind, I am heading to bed."

Argus inclined his head. "I will see you in class."

She smiled slightly and nodded.

Heading to her room seemed like the best thing for her to do. Hopefully, she wouldn't dream of panthers on fire.

Chapter Twelve

With the threat of the magic-sucker gone, the campus breathed a sigh of relief. Imara's name was kept out of the official reports, and no one on campus mentioned the familiar.

Life returned to the cycle of studying, tests, exams and spell work.

Tuesday lunches with Argus became a habit that they both enjoyed. The weeks flew by, and soon, there was only the exam left.

"So, one more class and I don't see you again?" She quirked her lips.

"You know that isn't true. I simply want to abide by your schedule, so let me know when you would like to go out for a meal or coffee, and if I am awake, I will be there."

She smirked. "Well, I do have time off between the terms. I will be starting again, but I have three weeks off after exams."

"So, after next week you have time off?"

"Yup, if the herbology exam doesn't turn me into something unfortunate."

"Are you worried?"

"Not really. After the way this term started, I have been practicing all of my magic skills and am confident that I can pass my courses."

He grinned. "I am confident as well. If I could read your handwriting, I would be tempted to cheat off your paper."

She laughed. "During the ethics test?"

"Yeah, it would be ironic."

She was still smiling a few minutes later, but it faded when she finally asked the question she needed to know. "Why did she do it?"

"Based on her journals, blog, and texts, she was assaulted the last term by someone at one of the frat houses. Her fury became the power that lashed out at others and women who were partying without drinking were tempting targets. She could dose them with what they thought was plain soda and simply corner them in the shadows."

"Did the others recover?"

"They are still recovering, but their magic is returning."

"That is a relief. One fatality was enough."

He nodded in agreement.

She twisted her lips. "So, since you have persistently bought my food, I thought I would get you something to remind you of me when you are back at work."

Argus leaned forward and raised his

brows. "What is it?"

She reached into her bag and brought out a precisely wrapped box about two inches long and three inches wide.

"Here." She tucked her hands under the table.

"Shall I open it?"

"Please. It is just something small."

He took the box, and it looked tiny in his hand. He pulled back the neat bow and popped open the side to slide the box free. When he opened the box, Mr. E sat up on her shoulder.

The enamelled metal black cat with huge green eyes looked up at Argus with smiling lips.

He grinned. "Thank you."

Without another word, he attached the keychain to his keys.

"There, whenever you see him, you will think of me."

He chuckled. "You are pretty firmly entrenched in my thoughts."

"I hate to say that I am pleased about that. Have Lio and Ivar gotten over my age?"

He wrinkled his nose. "They are working on it."

"I will get older."

"I know, and I will be waiting. Your mother isn't pleased with our interaction."

She laughed. "She is just going to make sure that you aren't a serial killer. One of those attached to me is enough."

Mr. E let out a mew and purred.

"Well, you need to study for the exam, and I want to fly around the campus. I will see you tomorrow, Argus, and I will miss you when you leave the campus entirely."

"Then, let me take you back to your hall, and you can get on with your flight. See you tomorrow for the exam."

She nodded. "Yup. Let's go."

They got up from their table at the

coffee shop, and Mr. E hopped onto her shoulder. It was amazing that he never got larger, but he was a projection of a kitten wrapped around a killer. It was best that he stayed the size that he was.

Their walk across campus was far slower than it needed to be, but she enjoyed it. The exams started the next day, and the rest of her week would be hell. This was the calm before the storm.

"Did you want to come in to do some cramming?" She quirked her lips as they approached the hall.

"No, I think I had better be on my way. I can't concentrate when you are around, my friend." Argus chuckled.

They used the words *my friend, buddy, dude, madam* to keep distance between them. It was working so far to remind them that nothing else could happen until she had graduated. They were holding tight to it.

When he left her at her door, she

went in to face a pile of books; Bara's loom in the study area was clicking away as she laughed with Reegar. Imara watched them for a moment before she joined in and settled at the study table with the hum of her companions around her. She had an exam in the morning, and she wanted to knock it out of the park.

The Magical Ethics exam had been gruelling. For the first time, Imara begged off going out with Argus, and she crept home for some rest.

She could see him again after she ran the gauntlet of exams. Two more and she would be ready for a well-deserved rest.

Bara and Reegar made her a tremendous breakfast on the day of her herbology exam. If she was going to have to drink her own potion, they didn't want it to happen on an empty stomach.

With her purse and familiar, she headed out to the exam lab, collected her pot of herbs from its secure locker, and she carried it to her workspace.

The proctors were watching the students, and four of them came over when she put her pot down on the table.

Her instructor checked the content of the pots using potions to test the magical transmission of the herbs.

Imara stood with her plants and watch the other students' offering be tested one by one. Only one student had zero magical effect in their herbs, the rest had sparks and crackling energy released by the testing potion.

When the magus stood in front of Imara, she wiped her palms on her thighs.

"What are those?"

She cleared her throat. "They appear

to be apples on a rosemary bush."

"I see. And these?"

"Basil."

"No, the small objects."

She leaned forward and looked at the soft green leaves hiding the small curving items. "Bananas?"

"I see." He beckoned to one of the proctors, and a large vessel was wheeled over. The magus pulled off one of the apples with a pair of tongs and set it on the bottom of the vessel, clamped the lid on and poured the detection potion into the top.

Imara covered her eyes as a fountain of light poured out of the miniscule hole in the lid. It continued for several minutes and formed tumbles of pastel mists on the ceiling.

The instructor looked at her and nodded, "So, that is one hundred percent. May I know where you got the soil?"

"It was on campus, and there is a paper trail for my permissions." She looked at the avid students on her left and right.

"Of course. We will discuss it later."

He moved on and continued testing until the remainder of the students demonstrated their horticultural leanings.

When the exam was over, she scooped up her pot and watched Mr. E playing with the leaves.

"Ms. Mirrin?"

"Yes, Magus?"

"May I keep your exam project?"

She blinked. "I don't think that would be appropriate, but you can take an apple and a banana."

He smiled brightly and nodded. "Thank you. That is a lot of energy."

"Yeah. I lucked into a hint, and it paid off."

"I will be in contact with you for the location."

"That would be fine. It would be best if you could come to the hall. That way I can be assured of privacy."

"Of course. Excellent. I will be in touch. This is a phenomenal result."

He got his samples, and she got her mark. With a swing in her step, she only had to face the final exam. Domestic Magic.

She faced the room and tried to figure out if she had missed anything. She had unclogged a drain, removed a spilled potion and its effects from a carpet, pulled a cursed object out from under a settee using a rubber glove, and cleared crumbs out of a cupboard with a compression spell.

The timer chimed, and she had to stand while the instructor investigated the chamber.

"You missed the window, but you got the cursed idol under the settee without activating it, so you have passed, Ms. Mirrin. Excellent job."

Imara sighed in relief.

"Thank you, am I free to go?"

"Yes, yes. I have to reset this for the next student."

She was waved off and left the testing chamber that she had been assigned. There were five chambers active, and all had staggered start times. She was glad it was over and done with.

Imara was exhausted. Her focus for the term was over, and she had a few weeks of blank thought ahead of her. Good, bad, or ugly, she was done.

Reegar Hall had never looked so welcome. She walked in and headed for the common space only to shriek in shock.

"Surprise!" Bara and Reegar were flanked by Luken, Lio, Ivar, and Argus. Near the cake, Mirrin was standing with a present.

"I can't believe you did this again."

Reegar chuckled. "You are only here for another year and a bit, so I am making the most of it. Small parties are the best ones."

She chuckled and hugged her way through her friends and family. Argus held on just a bit longer than was appropriate, but she didn't comment.

The cake excited Mr. E. A black kitten sitting on a spell book took front and centre. *I have never been depicted in sugar before. I am perversely honoured.*

Imara chuckled, cut the cake, and the party got into full swing.

The XIA agents were interrogating Luken, trying to find out why he hadn't been a proper big brother to her. When he finally admitted—loudly—that Imara was his elder, Reegar turned and stared at her.

She shrugged weakly and smiled. "I am usually in a hurry to get my way."

Argus grinned. "I will remember that."

For some reason, she blushed.

Mr. E had badgered her into protecting his image on the cake, and he was guarding it like it was his baby.

Liirick arrived around sunset, and he brought takeout. The party continued into the evening, and after hours of trying, Imara got away from the crowd and headed up to the roof.

She was unsurprised when Argus joined her after a few minutes, but she didn't mind.

"So, no familiar?"

"He is playing with his new icing friend."

Argus sighed and walked up to her, wrapping his arms around her from behind and staring out over the college with her.

"You are a force of nature, Imara."

"Nope. I just have a focus. My life has

been filled with an absence of hope, so I made it for myself. I am content with it."

"I am in awe."

"You are not. You are unsure because you haven't run into many women with this mindset."

He hugged her. "That too, but I am still impressed. I know where you came from, so to have your success is astonishing. I know you don't use magic to achieve it and that makes it all the more amazing."

"Well, I do use magic in the classes. That is what this college is about. I can't advertise myself as a spectral consulting magus if I am not a magus. I have to be registered with the guild, and that takes credentials."

"See? You have a plan to make something from nothing. You take my breath away."

He lowered his head to her neck for a kiss, and she smacked his forehead. "No shenanigans. Two more years."

He sighed. "Right. Two more years. You are just so sweet, lovely, intelligent, and powerful, I want to be with you at all times."

"Trust me, you are always in my thoughts, but I have my goals, and I will achieve them. When that is done, I can open my social options to include a partner." She patted his arm.

"As long as it is me, I can wait."

She grinned and watched the moon rising and the stars coming out. Argus kept her warm and simply held her as the sky performed just for them. The moment took her breath away.

Not all enchantments were magic.

Author's Note

Well, Imara is moving on and the next book, *Sky Breaking 301* will take her into weather manipulation and send her colliding with several of her brothers.

Mr. E will have a chance to pull on his hellkitten guise again, and Imara continues her journey to her professional life. Did you know that consulting for the XIA gets you college credit?

Look for the next instalment before the fall... but not much before. I have a very full dance card.

Thanks for reading,
Viola Grace

About the Author

Viola Grace (aka Zenina Masters) is a Canadian sci-fi/paranormal romance writer with ambitions to keep writing for the rest of her life. She specializes in short stories because of the thrill of discovery, of all those firsts, is what keeps her writing.

An artist who enjoys a story that catches you up, whirls you around and sets you down with a smile on your face is all she endeavours to be. She prefers to leave the drama to those who are better suited to it, she always goes for the cheap laugh.